# THE LAWMAN AND THE SONGBIRD

At Governor Edgerton's request, Pinkerton detective Joshua Dillard is sent to a lawless Montana boomtown peopled by avaricious gold prospectors and ruthless bandits. Joshua immediately sets his sights on the arrogant Blackie Dukes and his bunch. Then 'Aces' Axford's safe at the Magnet saloon is robbed right under Joshua's nose. It seems the gold has been spirited away by Axford's pretty employee Kate Thompson, who has also double-crossed the dangerous Dukes gang. Now, seven years later, Joshua returns to Montana as the town's marshal. It's time to solve the mysteries and lay a ghost to rest with a blazing six-shooter.

# THE LAWMAN AND THE SONGBIRD

# The Lawman And The Songbird

*by*

Chap O'Keefe

**Dales Large Print Books**
Long Preston, North Yorkshire,
BD23 4ND, England.

British Library Cataloguing in Publication Data.

O'Keefe, Chap
    The lawman and the songbird.

    A catalogue record of this book is
    available from the British Library

    ISBN   978-1-84262-547-7 pbk

First published in Great Britain in 2005
by Robert Hale Limited

Copyright © Chap O'Keefe 2005

Cover illustration © Gordon Crabb by arrangement with
Alison Eldred

The right of Chap O'Keefe to be identified as the author of this
work has been asserted by him in accordance with the
Copyright, Designs and Patents Act, 1988

Published in Large Print 2007 by arrangement with
Robert Hale Ltd.

Dales Large Print is an imprint of Library Magna Books Ltd.

Printed and bound in Great Britain by
T.J. (International) Ltd., Cornwall, PL28 8RW

# 1

## MURDER IN MONTANA

'I don't wanna die with m' boots on,' the gold panner gasped. The pain in his shattered, gunshot kneecaps was excruciating.

One of his tormentors waved a smoking Colt .44 revolver; kicked the crippled prospector in the ribs. 'To hell with your blasted boots! Tell us where you've hidden your stash.'

He looked around the rough-and-ready shack the man had thrown up: the walls made of axed alders and interwoven brush, the roof that was no more than two water-proof tarps tied down over more brush and alder string-pieces. His gang had already ripped apart the prospector's straw mattress and torn the lid off the chest where he kept his grub safe from the packrats.

He saw no other furnishings or obvious hidey-holes.

'C'mon, damn you, Pappy Jack, let's hear it!'

The hardcases' leader was lean and sinewy with greasy black hair. On his right thigh was the tied-down holster whence he'd drawn his fired Colt. The butt of another gun protruded from a shoulder holster worn under his right arm and a black leather vest. His dead-white face looked as cold and emotionless as a skull despite the vehemence in his words.

'Don't have no ... gold, Dukes,' the miner jerked out. 'The claim I got staked's a dud ... ain't seen more'n a speck or two o' colour in a month of pannin', I swear. All gravel an' black sand.'

He sighed gustily and his eyes fluttered shut.

'The old jackass's lyin', Blackie,' the youngest, most vicious member of the Dukes bunch told his leader. 'I seen him flash a full poke of dust and nuggets at the bar of the Magnet. An' all the territory knows the Broken Man Gulch diggings are the richest in Montana – mebbe in the whole goddamn nation.'

'Well, Billy McGee, you figure out how we make him tell,' Blackie Dukes said with a sneer. 'I do believe he's just passed out. Fetch a pan of water, kid.'

Pappy Jack's head had slumped to one side. Under a battered felt hat with a squashed high crown, his face was fish-belly grey. His eyes had not reopened.

'Naw!' Billy said. 'I reckon he's foxin', the sneaky ol' bastard. I'll soon wake him up jumpin' – just like I do the dudes in Cox City.'

The 'city' was the mining camp and boom town that had sprung up almost overnight after the discovery of gold in Broken Man Gulch. The kid had two favourite stunts, which he pulled when backed up by the older, wilier hellraisers in Blackie Dukes's gang. One was to ride his horse into the tent saloons and stores; the other was to shoot holes through gents' hats.

Being cocky and full of himself, Billy thought he cut an attractive figure on horse-back, especially to women, with his wavy brown hair, light-blue eyes and wiry if not muscular build. He was also very proud of his marksmanship.

Now he pulled out his revolver in the crowded shack, which caused his pards to shrink back from the line of fire between Billy and their slumped victim. The gun was a silver-plated Colt .44 with pearl handles and was tastefully engraved. With a half-bent elbow, Billy raised the showy weapon slightly in front of his lanky body at waist level. Sure of his aim, he squeezed the trigger.

The fiery crash was deafening in the shack, but without echo off the brush walls or roof.

To Billy's consternation, the shabby hat didn't sail off Pappy Jack's head. And the man, hat and all, keeled over completely.

'Christ!' snarled one of the bunch. 'I do

believe yuh've killed him, Billy boy. Now we'll never know where he's gotten his fortune salted away.'

Dukes poked at Pappy Jack with a black-booted toe. The bullet-holed hat rolled off.

The old prospector had a high, bald dome that had evidently reached further into the crumples of the hat's crown than Billy had judged. A fatal, bloody furrow had been carved through the bare scalp, exposing the grey and sanguineous contents in the cavity below.

'You've spilled ol' Jack's brains it seems, kid,' Dukes said. 'That was a crazy fool thing to have done.'

'Devilish,' another said. 'Hell of a note.'

'Ain't never happened to me before,' Billy blurted. 'Must've been on account of his having an unnatural head. What d'we do?'

Dukes shrugged. 'He's no use to us now. Drag his carcass outa here and take it down to the creek. Pitch it into the flow.'

'But it's broad daylight, Blackie.'

Another shrug. 'Makes no never mind,

kid. This is Cox City, Montana, ain't it? He's just another fool miner in patched overalls an' a dirty shirt. Sling him across a horse's back.'

Billy scowled. 'I feel a real idiot ... losing us all that loot.'

'Yeah, that does need some studying on.' Dukes fixed him with a beady, snake-like stare. 'And as luck has it, you'll mebbe get the chance to put it to rights.'

'How so?' the kid asked, trying to look eager rather than plain jelly-legged scared.

'You'll help us grab a haul of gold that'll make this broken-down bum's missing poke look like chickenfeed.'

'Where is it?'

Dukes' thin lips twitched in a creepy travesty of a smile. 'In Aces Axford's safe in his office at the Magnet.'

One of the others scoffed. 'We'd never get a crack at that, Blackie. 'Sides, what do we know 'bout opening safes?'

'We don't have to handle that personal, Lou. An' the kid's a natural for the part he has to handle. All he has to do is sweet-talk Kate Thompson into helping out and keeping her mouth shut.'

'Yuh mean that Magnet dance-hall gal the kid's been a-sparkin'?'

Dukes nodded the head that looked like living death. 'That, if you want to spare Billy the words a plainer man might use, is exactly the Kate I mean.'

The life of Joshua Dillard was not packed with conventional success. A New York lady taking chances once dared to call him a soldier of misfortune. Yet his 'failures' were such only in that they were experienced as financial losses. A righter of wrongs, he invariably brought death and destruction, where apt.

What Joshua was to remember as the Cox City songbird affair involved two so-called 'failures', separated by seven years but tied together by an almost identical cast and setting.

The first episode began when Joshua,

employed by the Allan Pinkerton National Detective Agency of Chicago, was summoned to the office of Boise 'Boss' Flagler, his supervisor.

Flagler scratched the bushy beard that fringed his chin. 'What, Joshua, do you know about Cox City, Montana?'

'Wide open, Boss,' Joshua said succinctly.

At this time he was a smart, well-groomed young man of abstemious habits, as he needed to be. 'Pinks' – Pinkerton agents – were handpicked with an insistence on high decorum. Under Mr Allan's code, they had to have no addiction to drink, smoking, card-playing, low dives or slang.

Joshua reflected more on Flagler's question about Cox City before adding, 'A hell-roaring boom town, I guess. Tents, board shanties, brush wickiups, umpteen saloons and dance halls ... a few false-fronted stores. No banks, no schools, no churches yet.'

Flagler nodded. 'Primitive, in short. Yet it's where they all want to be: the adventurous, the desperate ... the wicked.'

'No surprise in that, Boss. Broken Man Gulch is where the newest gold strike's said to be. We've seen it before. The crowds rolling in from all corners of the land, stark-mad with excitement and full of hopes and dreams. Many of the greenhorns will get fleeced; some will die violent deaths.'

'Right. You've got the picture, and it ain't pretty. Federal law has no presence in the Territory of Montana; the little order there is stems from miners' courts, set up by popular assent.'

Flagler sketched some history. Just before the Civil War, Pinkerton had thwarted a plot to assassinate Abraham Lincoln. He had then backed the Union, directing secret-service work.

In the West, gold was discovered in Dakota. The great mining camps resulted in an influx of people, in road building, commercial enterprise and agricultural production in nearby valleys. And the miners formed vigilante groups to combat bandit gangs like that led by Henry Plummer, ostensibly Sheriff of Bannack, a Democrat by political inclination, but also an outlaw.

In 1863, the need for more appropriate law prompted Washington's creation of the Territory of Idaho, and President Lincoln, a Republican, picked former Republican Congressman Sidney Edgerton to be its chief justice.

Edgerton was assigned to go to the capital, Lewiston, and set up courts authorized by the elected legislature of Idaho. But he never got there to be sworn in and do the work.

Maybe it was gold that lured him to other districts, where he and a nephew played their part in a lynch system of justice, administered by a vigilante committee. He then returned to Washington to persuade it to establish another new territory, Montana, with Bannack the capital and himself Governor.

'Now Edgerton has retained our agency under secret contract to look into the mayhem in Cox City,' Flagler finished. 'Remember, Edgerton is a one-time appointee of Lincoln and afforded Mr Allan's deepest respect.'

'I savvy the political niceties, Boss,' Joshua said. 'So I'm off to Cox City. Where I set up undercover as what? Another placer miner among the teeming masses?'

'No, Joshua, you'll not need a pick and shovel yet. Nor will we equip you with prospecting pan, rocker, long tom and sluice. In point of fact, you won't join the real gold-rush hopefuls.'

'I won't? Kinda hard to be inconspicuous if you aren't one of the crowd.'

Flagler disagreed with a shake of his head. 'Oft-times it's the hangers-on in these boom-town situations that swell the numbers and make the surer money. The storekeepers, the freighters, the saloon-men. The dance-hall girls.'

'And which will I be?'

'I suggest a professional gambler. Edgerton has a sympathizer called "Aces" Axford who's the big wheel in the town. He owns the fanciest saloon and gambling hall, the Magnet.'

Joshua smiled. 'Aces? Is that a name these days?'

'His parents called him Alvin, but only a fool calls him that now. He was a one-time high-stakes gambler himself, but he has risen in a sinful world after allegedly selling guns and whiskey to war-minded Utes. Howsoever, today no one mentions that either. Axford has the nod from Edgerton, who enjoyed the confidence of the President, who had the loyalty of Mr Allan.'

'Yeah,' Joshua said, with an even more crooked smile. 'We've been through that. Old political friendships. I saw Edgerton once – a grave-eyed man with a Roman nose.'

'I doubt you'll see Edgerton again. Bannack is a way from Cox City. Rumour has it, too, that the Governor is on the point of resigning to return home to Ohio. He's a rich man, his fortune made from interests in seventy-five mining claims and other investments in the territory. I figure he views cleaning up Cox City as a kinda payoff to Axford.'

Joshua's comment was guarded. 'Hmm. I don't know that I entirely cotton to this Aces Axford. His prosperity and his allegiances already have a stink to them, even though Montana be ever so far...'

# 2

## BOOM-TOWN GIRL

'Drink up, Billy dear, and buy us both another,' Kate Thompson said. She had an enticing smile and bright, grey-green eyes, and a freshness that didn't seem to fit with gaudy, saloon-girl attire.

'Aw, yuh don't have to take that tone with me, Kate,' Billy McGee said, winking. 'That's fer the suckers. We're pards, ain't we?'

'Hush! The barkeeper might hear and Axford's spying on us from the stairs.'

'The smarmy rooster!' Billy hissed. 'Well, we're gonna show 'im, ain't we, gal?'

'Sure, Billy, but I do think you should buy more drinks. Otherwise, Axford's going to order me to spend less time with you. Or else he might insist I pursue our friendship in private in an upstairs room.'

Billy chuckled evilly. 'I'd be all for that.'

'I don't know that Blackie Dukes would agree,' Kate lied. 'It could get you noticed, and rooms cost a half-eagle an hour.'

Billy glanced over his shoulder. Saloon-man Aces Axford was a stocky gent dressed like a big-city dude in a cutaway coat with a silk handkerchief in a breast pocket, checked trousers and flowered vest. He smoked a cheroot and was well-barbered with waves in his hair and a curved, waxed moustache. He sported rings on several fingers and a big diamond pin in his tie.

Turning back, the kid growled, 'Robber! Fancy Dan!' Then, louder, 'Hey, 'keep! How 'bout some more drinks here?'

Kate Thompson was a roamer, and her roaming was ruled not by whim but by an occupation she hesitated to regard as her profession. That could be too grand or too downright demeaning.

Her places of work were dance halls and saloons and occasionally theatres. Frequently these businesses were housed in no more than the tents of boom towns.

At a young age, Kate had been orphaned and left in the care of a maiden aunt. The resentful aunt had shown her no affection and provided a home that was merely an unpaying workplace. While still poised between girlhood and womanhood, she'd run off and been lured, in her innocence, into becoming a dancer, a singer, a hostess ... whatever would keep the monetary wolf from the door, though often not the human wolves.

Always, Kate was an actress. To a greater or lesser degree, simulation allowed her to maintain the magic of her beauty and kept her from the destiny of many of her kind. This was to take the tempting few steps into becoming an 'upstairs girl', which, paradoxically, involved descent from the day's standards of purity; a surrendering of the maidenhood hypocritically held by society to be so important. Upstairs girls did not rise: they were fallen women, soiled doves.

Brave Kate was helped by a good soprano singing voice. Also, her stage-dancing talent extended beyond the ability to kick her toes to chin height while showing off frilly petticoats, black-stockinged legs and garters.

Sweet, but not totally innocent, dark-haired, under twenty, Kate was a type scarce in the frontier West. Few who answered the call of the boom towns stayed so lovely so long. She moved on to the next point of urbanization – be its mushroom growth stimulated by cattle trail, railroad-building or mining – whenever the pressures built and her tightrope stance became untenable. Her few possessions went along in one battered valise.

The present time found her in Montana and Cox City, a tatterdemalion settlement as any she'd seen, a place of rutted streets slightly away from the main diggings but full of the gold-rush bustle. The site was pocketed in lonely hills, bordering on mountainous. Often a bleak wind blew. In summer, it baked under the sun; in winter, it was piled with snowdrifts. Once the sun dropped behind the Bitterroots, long shadows made it sombre and depressing.

Tents and shanties were everywhere, but there were some frame buildings of more than one storey, a few structures based on brick and stone, and many stores that had quickly jacked but imposing false-fronts of unmatching lumber. A livery barn had been well founded. Saloons, gambling halls, dance halls and liquor stores outnumbered all other enterprises. Openly, on the fringe of the brave 'city', were houses and tents of prostitution.

But most confident and substantial of all the centres of attraction was the rightly named Magnet, where money and whiskey flowed like water.

It was here Kate was engaged in her multi-talented capacity, but chiefly as part of a cancan-dancing chorus line of six, and for her abilities, when the show was over, to inveigle the hugely disproportionate male clientele into buying more drinks than were good for their heads, bodies or pockets.

A hundred-foot bar was in place – mahogany with brass fittings. It had scales for weighing gold dust and was backed by the mirror customary in the best watering-holes. But Gulch gossip had it the two-storeyed, block-long Magnet would soon sport all the fancy trimmings its roistering patrons could imagine, freighted in at adventurous expense. The walls would display oil paintings of voluptuous nudes and chandeliers would hang over the dance floor. A platform already accommodated musicians, piano, fiddles and banjoes, and the stage shows.

Games of chance – poker, blackjack, faro and dice – supplied a constant click and rattle, punctuated by the occasional whoop of delight or groan of dismay.

A staircase led to a gallery, off which doors gave access to private rooms where it was said a man could take his pleasure with the cleanest girls in Montana.

Everywhere, under a haze of smoke, was the reek of rich cigars and cheroots and the sweat of the revellers.

The man behind this display of substance was Aces Axford. This moment he was keeping an eagle eye on the bustle. Kate was aware of him in the shadows at the head of the gallery stairs, watching as she kept company at the bar with Billy McGee.

Kate found Billy McGee handsome enough as callow youths went. But he had too high an opinion of himself and his blue eyes were peculiarly cold, suggesting to her that at bottom a streak of vicious, conscienceless cruelty ran through him.

It was helpful that he thought himself in command of the situation, little knowing that her knowledge of men and their ways far outweighed his understanding of women, which he rashly considered complete.

Billy believed he'd befriended Kate, but it was she who'd encouraged him. She knew he was a young associate of the bullying Blackie Dukes, who was widely suspected of all manner of profitable criminality around Cox City, but whom no one in the lawless community was bold enough to brace or even expose with evidence of his gang's nefarious doings.

Kate had gained Billy McGee's confidence with her innocent and winsome manner, knowing men soon became braggarts when they were around women they wanted to impress. She lured him on, led him to boast, so that he'd spilled the Dukes bunch's plans and was now recruiting her as their assistant.

These plans featured Aces Axford as victim.

Kate rightly had no sympathy for her employer, or any other member of Axford's parasitic breed. She'd known many in her adolescent and adult years; she didn't want to spend the rest of life meeting more.

The time had come to screw up courage and break away from a path that would inevitably turn downward. What Kate had in mind included not only robbing Axford, but double-crossing her partners in the scheme. A dangerous goal indeed.

Over fresh drinks – Kate's discreetly watered down according to Axford's standing instructions, by an obnoxious barkeep – she and Billy quietly discussed Dukes's grand plot. Kate hoisted her short skirt a mite more, and they put their heads close together like a pair of lovebirds. Or a working girl negotiating with a dirty-talking prospective client.

'It's damn nigh all fixed,' Billy whispered, his unsettling eyes peering into the cleavage presented by her low-cut, up-thrusting, red sateen bodice. 'Fingers O'Malley's hit town. Come as a prospector, o' course. But Blackie knows he was a safebreaker in New York.'

'Oh, how exciting!' Kate gushed *sotto voce*, while contemplating with slight amazement how easy it was for a woman to worm her way into knowing every secret of a distracted man. 'And am I going to be his helper?'

'Sure. Blackie Dukes says you'll sneak outa the gals' dressin'-room an' unbolt the door into the side alley where it'll be full dark. O'Malley'll be waitin'. Yuh'll show him in, an' take him up to Axford's office. That's it. He does the rest.'

Kate frowned. 'But what if Axford comes? What if someone hears? Or notices my odd behaviour?'

'Don't yuh worry none, sweet thing. Blackie an' me – with the rest of the gang kinda pitchin' in – are gonna be holdin' up the bar right here as a diversion. It'll be a real ruckus, guns firin', men shoutin', women screamin'. Nobody'll get a chance to think of anythin' else. I tell yuh, Blackie says it'll go smooth as a stiff peeder in an' out a wet whore.'

Like the green kid he was, he thought to impress her with his bawdy man-talk. Though she found it offensive, Kate was also

28

reassured. Here was the best chance she'd ever had of quitting the hopeless cycle of one risky job after another until the time finally came when she was ravished and put on the road to ruin.

'It sounds just dandy, but you can't blame a girl for fretting.' She shivered and let her grey-green gaze travel the busy room.

When it met that of a man dealing at a baize-covered, card-decorated table, momentary confusion caused her to lower her face. Kate had an eye for detail and was an excellent observer. She'd seen this man watching her before, especially when her companion was Billy. His name was James Danford and he was said to be an old gambling friend of Aces Axford.

She judged that unlikely somehow.

Mr Danford's dedication to the tables was not complete. She'd seen him strolling, as though inquisitively peering into Cox City's ramshackle buildings, and roving as far as the unclaimed, weed-grown lots and the frenetic-ally busy diggings, which the true gambler would have regarded with contempt.

His hands shuffled cards expertly enough, pouring a deck from one to the other so swiftly that the riffling sound was like the song of a saw through dry wood. His trade was signalled by fashionable, mail-order Eastern clothes, and his long, dextrous fingers fitted him for his part.

But the professional gamblers she'd encountered before had all been denoted by a kind of fatalism. Though very courteous, even gallant, they'd been pasty, hard-faced indoor adventurers – bluntly, cold-blooded card-sharps with not an ember of warmth in their hearts. And their eyes had been dead eyes.

Axford's 'friend' had clear blue eyes, alive and steady, with an assessing challenge that caused her composure to slip.

So the dealing was a front for what?

All manner of men had been drawn to the Gulch, and thence the Magnet. She'd met veterans from the California goldfields, farm boys from New England, renegade soldiers, trappers and mountain men, doctors and lawyers – some forsaking their calling and others attempting to pursue it.

Yet this James Danford above all others made Kate uneasy. How would his interest affect her daring plotting?

Joshua Dillard watched the pretty saloon girl tête-à-tête with Billy McGee. It wasn't the first time he'd seen her chatting with him. They seemed to have gotten mighty close while he'd had the members of the Dukes bunch under observation as prime suspects for the robberies and murders rife in the Gulch. McGee, of course, spent half their time together checking his own reflection in the back-bar mirror. But for the moment, in a public place and dressed as skimpily as the girl was, they could scarcely be closer without causing an uproar.

Eventually, Axford came down the stairs and threaded his way through the crowded gaming tables and smoke-thick atmosphere. Joshua caught his eye, and made a beckoning movement with his head. Spectators stood before Joshua's faro layout two and three deep, but they parted respectfully when Axford shouldered his way between them.

'A word with you when I may, Mr Axford,' Joshua murmured.

'Why, certainly, Mr Danford, in my office. I'll send someone over to work the table.'

The punters bought their checks, or markers, from Joshua and made bets by placing them directly on the thirteen card ranks glued on the playing table. Joshua slid cards from his spring-loaded box, saw checks won and lost.

Working as a house dealer was a fine but sometimes demanding cover. Faro was complicated, in scoring, betting and vocabulary. Finally, Joshua had dealt from soda to hock – first card to last. He was able to hand over to another and leave his post.

He made his way from a door behind a velvet curtain into the gloomy passages between the back rooms. Behind the scenes, the Magnet made no pretence at grandeur, until you entered Axford's private office, where the boom-town impresario had spent money on his comforts.

Axford, lounging in a padded swivel chair behind a solid desk, gestured to a liquor cabinet. Finger rings glittered. 'Help yourself to a drink, Dillard, and tell me what's on your mind.'

'A couple of things, Mr Axford,' Joshua said. He flexed his shoulders and twisted his neck to stretch tired muscles before he picked up the heavy, cut-glass decanter.

'Aces, my boy, Aces.'

'It seems to me – Aces, that one of your girls is spending a heap of time with Billy McGee, a member of the Dukes gang.'

'Yeah, I seen that myself. Kate Thompson, right fetching gal. Pay no mind. She's only doing her job. No one can pin anything on Dukes, let alone his hangers-on. And Miss Kate encourages young McGee to buy a lot of liquor.'

'I think it might go somewhat further than that.'

Axford was dismissive. 'So what if the kid's on fire for her? I'd admire to get the filly alone myself, but she ain't open to that stuff yet. Mark you, when she does decide to grant the whippersnapper her favours, there'll be a cut owing the house.'

Joshua shrugged. In the Gulch, Axford represented the agency's client. It wasn't for him to argue. The whiskey was balm on the throat and spread warming tentacles through his belly.

'And this other thing, Joshua?'

Swirling what was left in his glass of Axford's high-quality imported malt, Joshua said, 'I've been trained to have a good memory for faces, and I saw one in town today I think I ought to have known. Unfortunately, I still can't put a name to it, though I believe the agency has a mugshot of the feller.'

'Mugshot? What's that?'

'A Pinkerton innovation, Mr – Aces. As criminals and crimes make the newspapers, our field agents diligently clip every report and send them in to our offices. Folders on criminals with their pictures, or mugshots, remain in the central files until the person is dead. The practice is spreading to police forces.'

Axford gave a twisted grin. 'Well, villains of every stripe answer the lure of gold. And the West has always been a great place for fellers out to make a fresh start, no questions asked.'

'That's true. But I kinda have an intuition this man's presence has significance. Without facts or logic, that might sound unreasonable coming from a detective. But I'll try describing him to my supervisor. Maybe he can mail me copies of pictures that match, together with records.'

Joshua put down his empty glass and punched a closed fist into the palm of his other hand. 'I just hope it won't be too late to help.'

Axford laughed. 'Help what, Dillard?'

# 3

## THE DOUBLE-CROSS

Kate Thompson needed an accomplice. She chose a co-worker, Hannah Powell. While Kate had a room at the hotel next to the Magnet no bigger than a closet, Hannah could just afford the rent for a log-and-clapboard cabin on the edge of town. Others had shunned it because it was beneath their dignity to live neighbouring the settlement's red-light district.

'You could do the same, Kate,' she said. 'Aces is always pesterin' me to give you ridin' lessons. Fornication's the only way a spinster gal can make a fortune in a town like this.'

'No. Hannah, I couldn't.' The cabin was cosy, but Kate shivered. Though she knew a girl's life and body should be her own – that what she chose to do with them was none of anyone's business – she felt depressed.

'Virtue's for fools,' Hannah said bluntly. 'We should take the goddamn horny bastards for ev'ry ounce of gold they got. Once you'd gotten initiated, you'd do swell with your looks – have an easier lot. And without a word of a lie, a gal does get to like it some.'

Hannah was several years Kate's senior ... mid-twenties and past the prime of her beauty, though remnants of it persisted beneath the rouge on her cheeks and the kohl on her eyelids. Lines etched about eyes and mouth, a bloating of breasts and broadening of hips, attested to a slide into hardness more than age. By Kate's reading of the evidence in herself and Hannah, enticing men to buy drinks took less toll than making your body available to their boozy invasions in upstairs rooms.

Hannah was a soiled dove ... outside of which she was a loyal friend and meant well. Though not fiction's absurd whore with a heart of gold, she had a patience and a capacity to endure the rigours of her career. Practised at all the come-hither wiles, she'd passed on many of the arts to Kate – those, that is, her young pupil had cared to learn. But her chin sometimes tended to quiver under stress, betraying the fundamental vulnerability of one of her kind in the woman-starved territories.

Hannah also had a weakness for liquor curbed only by her income and the Magnet's watering-down of its girls' drinks.

Kate pressed on to the purpose of her visit.

'Hannah, I can't be as accepting as you of all the things being a saloon girl entails. But I do mean to help us both, and I'm not scared of – facing dangers, though different ones from those you run.'

Kate told her what she'd learned from Billy McGee.

Hannah was sceptical. 'So you're gonna help them rob Aces Axford's safe. Maybe they'll give you some of the pickings; maybe they won't. I know the meanness of Blackie

Dukes. Luck, Kate.'

'I don't intend they should lay their hands on any of the pickings,' Kate said. 'When the gang holds up the bar, my idea is that they'll walk into a trap. I'll have slipped an anonymous message to the Bannack sheriff's deputy in Cox City. You know, Steve Wye. It'll tell about the raid on the saloon, but say nothing about the office break-in. Dukes, McGee and the rest will be caught red-handed.'

'So who gets Axford's hoard? This Fingers O'Malley?'

'Of course not. *We* do.'

Hannah's brows knitted. 'Us? How do you figure that out?'

'I'm pulling a double-cross on the lot of them. You've got a strong arm, Hannah. When O'Malley and I come out of Axford's office with the stuff from the safe, you'll be waiting beside the door in the dark of the passage. You'll slug him with a sand-filled pouch we'll have gotten ready for the purpose.'

'You're plumb crazy, Kate! If Dukes an' his boys can't come after us, later on Axford and Deputy Wye will.' She was tearfully concerned by the prospect. 'How can you be so stupid? They'll make this O'Malley sing to save his hide.'

'No one will see you, Hannah – not even O'Malley. We'll split the haul and I'll promptly hightail it out of Cox City and this life forever. If anyone does question you – because you were my friend – you'll know nothing. Certainly not where I've headed; *that* I'm not going to tell you. When it's learned I've vanished, everyone will think it was just Kate Thompson, and that all the loot has gone with me.'

Hannah shook her head and wrung her hands, saying nothing.

Then Kate produced a bottle of the Magnet's cheapest redeye from a pocket in her skirt and offered it. 'Maybe you should have a drink. I admit it's a bit startling.'

Hands shaking, Hannah took the bottle, placed it to her trembling lips and tipped.

'You're a smart 'un, Kate, I can't argue 'bout that...'

'So you're going to help me then?'

'I didn't say that. I'm thinkin' on it.'

But Kate knew Hannah through and through. She could count on Hannah's allegiance and her courage, boosted though it might have to be by raw liquor. Hannah's answer was already yes.

'The letter was thrown through my window in an old poke with a rock in it,' Deputy Steve Wye told Joshua Dillard, who'd been summoned by Aces Axford to his office.

Joshua distrusted Axford's visitor. No better than any individual riding the wave of the gold rush, Wye considered himself a cut above other men in Cox City of greater experience and probity. A *lawman*. But his high opinion was backed merely by a badge. His first, it had been pinned on him scant months ago by a sheriff in Bannack who was probably a crook.

He knew nothing of detection and was

familiar with criminal activity only in as much as it coincided with his own inbred slyness and trickiness. Joshua regretted Axford had taken the man into his confidence, betraying his (Joshua's) identity to him.

Joshua had a suspicion 'Wye' wasn't his real name, either. That was probably something unpronounceable, an East European name, judging by the man's Slav looks, and maybe beginning with a letter Y.

'Didn't you see who threw the poke, Wye?' Joshua asked. 'And where is the poke? And the rock for that matter?'

'You Pinks are too damn smart, mister,' Wye said, his face darkening. 'I brought Aces the letter, didn't I? The poke was a bit of rubbish; the rock, a rock. I tossed 'em in the river. And how could a man see who chucked the stuff? It was dark and I had the burlap across my window.'

Axford made placating noises. 'Now then, gents. Maybe this hasn't been played out the ideal way. But we'll nail Dukes and company this time, if the unsigned letter's true.

Maybe we can keep our eyes and ears open to learn more about the writer.'

'Fat chance,' Joshua murmured.

'Can we be done with this, Dillard?' Wye said. 'I got us a time and date for the stick-up, ain't I? Me and Aces'll have the place filled with armed men ready to stop it.'

'Sure we will, Deputy,' Axford said. 'We can let you go about your business now, but thanks for bringing me the letter.'

Dismissed by his shots-calling host, Wye stamped out, still bristling, still convinced of his own superiority.

'Decide what you want, Dillard, like Aces has done, and I'll fix it for you.'

'Jesus, what a prickly, stupid bastard!' Joshua said, shaking his head in disgust.

Axford sat back in his chair and waved a hand. Tendrils of acrid blue cheroot smoke were cast adrift to augment the fug lit by the shaded lamp that stood on his desk.

'Well, he's enthusiastic. There's a lot of stuff I don't 'preciate, too, but I'm seasoned enough to realize I don't know it all. So I try to keep my eyes open to learn more, then push when I'm fairly confident of the ground I'm standing on. I reckon Steve is excited about being a sheriff's deputy, and is trying to do his duty to the best of his ability. For a fact, he doesn't have the extensive background in detectiving you Pinks have. He's a tenderfoot. I'm willing to forgive that unless things get messy.'

Joshua sighed. He feared Wye was the kind of self-appointed expert likely to trigger a disaster for everyone while nurturing a personal reputation he'd never deserve. Clearly he was jealous of Joshua for the attention given him by Cox City's kingpin.

'You're too kind, Aces. Pass me the letter, will you?' Axford obliged and Joshua sniffed at the paper, smoothed out the crumples and peered at the writing.

*Mr Wye*

*Please be aware that Mr Blackie Dukes and his associates will hold up the bar of the Magnet on Saturday night.*

He sat silent and thoughtful for long seconds before revealing his conclusions.

'The notepaper's ordinary stock,' he said, 'but I reckon it might still have a lingering trace of a woman's perfume about it, despite the clumsy way that oaf's treated it. The hand is very neat, too – copperplate – and in a typically womanish style.'

Axford looked pleased. 'Uh-huh! That narrows it considerable, there being many more men than women in Broken Man Gulch.'

'But still too many to collect writing samples, Aces. Too, when a thing is prepared with such precision and care, it can be that the hand is specially assumed or copied. Disguised.'

Joshua was about to add to his analysis; to say why it was his hunch none of this mattered here. But he didn't. Even in these comparatively early days of his career, shrewdness was ingrained. He had an instinct for sensing coming trouble and knowing what course of action was likely to be in the best interests of justice and fair play. Which meant he didn't entirely subscribe to the Pinkerton ethic in every case. Already he was his own man with his own ideas, willing to buck the rules.

From his observations, he had a notion who might have written the letter, but for now he planned to go about that part of the business by the dictates of Dillard-style reasoning.

Thus he said no more to Aces Axford.

An unexpected blow fell before the week was out. Joshua found himself addressed by all and sundry as Dillard, or even familiarly as Joshua. His *nom de guerre* was scarcely to be heard.

The carefully built cover as Mr James Danford, faro dealer, was blown. It was also voiced around that the mysterious Joshua Dillard worked for the 'Pinks'.

The Pinkertons, who had a reputation for square dealing that even some outlaws recognized, rarely faced a critical press. But in a place as wide open as Cox City, Joshua would have preferred not to have been exposed to the distracting dangers of his profession. Among the riffraff attracted by the diggings were many of the criminal fraternity who might have vengeful cause to wish a representative of the agency dead.

At this juncture, it was an unwelcome complication.

Joshua spotted Steve Wye on the rutted main street, threading his way through the jostle of a bunch of new arrivals. He reached out and grabbed his arm. 'I want a parley with you.'

'What is this, Dillard?' Wye said, in a guttural voice.

'You just said it, Deputy. *Dillard*. We'll go along to your shack.'

He took a tighter grip, spun Wye around and effectively frogmarched him via the creek bank to his dwelling. Getting there, he flung open the door. The shack was furnished with drygoods boxes for table and chairs. It also had a bunk with a pole bottom and dried grass and sage stems for a mattress.

Joshua shoved Wye in, swung the door shut, then propelled him forward with a hard kick applied to the seat of his pants.

With a cry of indignation, Wye stumbled face-first on to his rude bunk. 'Hey! What is this? I don't unnerstand–'

'The hell you don't, you skunk,' Joshua said sourly. Wye was rubbing his bruised arm; Joshua took a bunch of his shirt in his hand and hauled him up.

'It's about putting my real name and job around.'

Fear or hatred, maybe both, came into Wye's eyes. Guilt had already been there. 'Uh ... well,' he began, stammering, 'I guess your alias slipped my mind.'

'Yeah,' Joshua jeered. 'Like everything slips your mind 'cept pushing your own goddamn interests.'

Wye struggled and regained a modicum of his cockiness. 'You can't do nothin' to me. I forgot you went by James Danford,' he maintained.

'You're a liar. The harm's been done, but I'm giving you some advice – the best you're apt to get in Cox City. If you're smart, you'll heed it and save yourself a lot of pain. I can't abide petty treachery. Any more and I'll crush you like I'd stomp on a cockroach – tin badge or no tin badge, Mr Wye.'

Joshua flung him down on the bunk with enough force to displace the crude bedding and send the breath whistling out of his mouth. He rapped a final contemptuous curse, turned on his heel and strode out. All brisk and impressively purposeful.

He'd let off some steam and issued a warning. He hoped it would be enough.

# 4

## BIG-NIGHT BLOOD-LETTING

Saturday night and the Magnet was jumping. Miners who stuck to traditional patterns of life fixed on ending a long week's work with celebratory abandon on the dance floor.

'Take your partners, please!' a master of ceremonies shouted. It was a dollar a throw to whirl your chosen girl. If you were a prospector, they weighed out your dust on the bar scales and you were given a ticket.

On the platform, a fiddler with one foot up on a chair made a scraping sweep with his bow; banjoes and a tinny piano took their cues and joined in. The caller sing-songed figures with a nasal twang. 'Gents all right a-heel an' toeing! Swing 'em, kiss 'em if you kin!'

What was it called? A quadrille? Joshua thought it all looked innocent enough – insofar as inaugural steps with a dove could be – but he felt the tension in the air. Stationed strategically throughout the big hall were trusted, armed miners recruited by Deputy Steve Wye and Aces Axford to foil the forecasted attempt to stick-up the bar.

He was taking a break from the faro dealing and could let his gaze rove the room. He found Kate Thompson, standing in a shadowed corner close to a door by herself, which was unexpected since she was an exceptionally pretty girl in a place so short of females that a man was apt to consider any girl, even the homeliest, worthy of attention. He guessed she was keeping herself apart deliberately.

But why so? Because Billy McGee was absent, maybe even now preparing with his sidekicks to swoop on the Magnet?

Joshua still didn't accept Aces Axford's contention that the relationship was insignificant; that the girl kept young McGee's company in the cause of selling drinks. Maybe she really had taken a shine to him and was missing him now. Or maybe she made out that she got along with him for some other reason...

Could she be their informant? What would she do when the raid took place? Would she help the gang, or...? Joshua would watch closely.

A saloon was one hell of a place for a showdown, but it had been decided, largely by Axford, that the raiders should be allowed right up to the bar. Then the 'keeps would drop behind its solid mass and the defenders of the peace would pen the bandits in from behind.

'Better than a running gunfight out on the street. Some of 'em would get clean away,' said Axford. He could be right.

Joshua wasn't left long into the big night to ponder the possibilities. Nor was there any mistaking when the raid began.

No fewer than ten hooded figures in long,

concealing, linen dusters crowded through the batwing doors, tearing both from their hinges in their forceful haste. They were armed with drawn pistols pointed aloft and announced their arrival with a sudden volley of firing – put .45 shells into the ceiling or whatever targets grabbed their fancy. Chunks of plaster fell, bottles smashed, a window fell out with a crash.

The revelry came to an abrupt halt. A woman screamed. A fiddler finished abruptly on a high, discordant note. The jangly piano tinkled to a halt.

Axford spat out the end of the cheroot he'd been chewing. 'Take cover! Keep your heads down, everybody!' he bawled.

Then Deputy Steve Wye lost his head and jumped his cue.

Joshua was himself startled at the size of the gang Dukes – if it was Dukes – had put together for the venture. The saloon's take, divvied up ten ways, wouldn't amount to that much. But the numbers were no reason to depart from plan, which was to let the raiders come right on in – far enough for most of them to be ambushed by a forewarned reception committee equipped with heavy revolvers and well-stocked cartridge belts.

Even so, another shot crashed out; a tongue of flame shot from the muzzle of the gun Wye had jerked from his holster, drawing and firing in a single motion. Joshua didn't see where the wild bullet lodged. Nowhere to do any good.

In an instant, the set-up dissolved into bedlam too fast to follow. Wye's fool stunt, quite beyond Joshua's or anyone's ability to foretell, had triggered a nightmare. Guns boomed in unison. Slugs whined about like angry hornets, gouging chunks from walls and furniture.

A gallant miner shoved a saloon girl to the floor, spread his arms and fell on top of her to shield her with his body. Their position was one with which she was doubtless familiar, though its reason was novel.

Two of the raiders went down with rapidly spreading splotches of blood on their dusters.

They lay groaning on the floor, one doubled up and clutching his belly.

One of Wye's miner crew, with blinding blood streaming into his eyes from a head wound, reeled into a post supporting the gallery, clutched it and kept saying, over and over, 'Oh my God! Oh my God!'

Judging by the cries and women's screams, innocent patrons were hit, too.

All these things and others Joshua witnessed only as blurred impressions. Clawing out his own gun, he ducked behind a table, even as lead chipped splinters off it just above his head. He cursed Wye under his breath.

'Stop the shooting!' he yelled, when a moment's respite hushed the din. 'Let's make a deal!' He knew the suggestion was damn' silly the moment he made it.

'Not on your life, by God!' a hood-muffled voice snarled back.

The air turned blue with both sides' blasphemies and profanity, gunsmoke swirled and the ruckus raged on unabated.

As soon as the hooded gunmen shoved through the batwings, Kate Thompson took off. She went through the internal door behind her, turning the key she'd previously placed in its lock.

The waiting had made her nervous. Too, she didn't think she'd imagined the measuring looks cast her way by the man she lately understood to be a Pinkerton detective. What slip could she have made to claim his attention? Activity was a part-cure, and Joshua Dillard's attention would now be occupied, surely?

The passage she'd entered was unlit. What light there was came from a transom window above the door at its far end. She took hurried steps to the door, where she drew two heavy bolts and lifted the latch.

She winced when she heard gunfire break out in the saloon behind her. It was more than she'd expected, and so soon. Such sustained shooting seemed unlikely to be in Blackie Dukes's plan.

A man pushed in through the door she'd

unlocked, clutching a rolled sack. He was a skinny little runt. He ignored her politely questioning, 'Mr O'Malley?' with a snap like a cur-dog's bark.

'Come on, gal – the safe! We ain't got all night.'

Over his shoulder, Kate made out Hannah Powell lurking at the narrow mouth of the alley. It was a small relief. One of her big fears had been that her accomplice would get cold feet and fail to show, although she'd slipped her a filched bottle of Axford's most drinkable whiskey to bolster her courage.

She led O'Malley in the dark to Axford's office. The door was locked, but the mechanism was primitive and delayed Fingers O'Malley's metal probe scant seconds.

'Kids' play. Why do the idiots bother?' he said, sneering at Kate as though she was personally responsible for the flimsy obstacle to his entry.

Men's angry shouts and the screams of women punctuated another exchange of gunfire in the saloon. Kate's heart was thumping wildly. Something had to have gone wrong. Were people being killed? How many more minutes would they have?

How long would it take O'Malley to crack the safe?

Kate lit the desk lamp while O'Malley unrolled his sack and went down on his knees in front of the safe. She thought he looked like he was about to pray.

'Be Lewis Lillie's work, this little beauty,' the ex-New York cracksman muttered. 'Cast-iron, with one of Linus Yale's new "Magic Locks". Philadelphia notion.'

'I'm sorry. I don't know the combination–' Kate began.

'Shuddup, gal. I gotta *hear* this thing. Weren't talkin' to you. Just meself.'

O'Malley worked at the lock with extraordinary long fingers as thin and sensitive-looking as any fine lady's. She saw how he'd gotten his nickname. He recited numbers to himself in a whispery sing-song. A tumbler fell into place at each breathless pause, till the door swung open.

'Nothing to it,' he said. 'Easy as a cracker box.'

Kate was amazed at how easy and quick it had been.

He thrust his arms inside the safe and raked out the stored pouches into his sack. Kate knew they'd be full of gold – dust or hundreds of nuggets. Even pea-size ones were worth a whole dollar. Helping him pack them into the sack, she noticed each of the pouches had a slip of paper stuffed into its closed neck.

O'Malley chortled. 'Thousands, gal, thousands, in the bag.' He hefted the sack to a scrawny shoulder; made for the door.

Kate hoped that Hannah wouldn't have been scared off by the continued sounds of battle from the saloon, and would be hiding alongside it, ready to strike O'Malley a knockout blow.

She willed her to be there.

To Joshua's mind the hooded gang seemed battered and disorganized, with two men down. The saloon's defenders, being prepared, had control of what was available in the way of cover: the gaming tables, the stairs, the long bar counter.

The robbery was not proceeding, but the outlaws blazed away with their revolvers every time anyone moved.

The turning point came when deputy Wye, foolhardy as he was, ducked out from under the stairway, flourishing his revolver. The move sparked an instant response. Joshua heard at least three cracking reports as guns were fired. One was Wye's, one was a bandit's, the other was Aces Axford's.

From the corner of his eye, Joshua saw Axford rise up from behind a corner of the musicians' stage. It looked like the slick sonofabitch was coolly drawing a bead with a revolver, easing back the hammer, but Joshua had no special reason to believe that the saloon owner had any great prowess with a six-shooter, and it was in the man's nature to do everything showy fashion.

When Axford cut loose, adding his contribution to the renewed pandemonium, his arm seemed to jerk, or swing, and Joshua thought it was Wye who copped his lead.

The impact of the heavy bullet knocked Wye off balance. He stumbled forward several steps into a sturdy chair. His body folded over its low, polished back. His eyes were wide and he attempted to speak. But all that came from his mouth was an agonized croak followed by a trickle, then a coughing explosion of dark blood.

Consternation and dismay rippled through the saloon crowd. Few could figure who had shot at whom or what, but their peace officer was down.

The bandits seized their chance. 'Outa here, men!' the leader roared, and they quit the saloon. Most exited through its doors, but one threw himself through a big front window. The glass crashed into a sparkling shower of smithereens and he was followed by two others.

Wye's stunned helpers rushed to give him aid Joshua could see he was beyond. He had bloody wounds in back and chest. And to Joshua's expert glance the latter looked like the exit wound.

But his sweeping eye was already moving on. Through the jagged opening in the broken front window, he saw the hooded men unhitch reins from posts and rails, mount up and lash horses away helter-skelter down the main stem. Their revolvers blazed to deter pursuit. Joshua refocused on the room. Something was missing...

Kate Thompson, the saloon girl, who'd been standing in the shadows by a rear door!

# 5

## HELL TO PAY

During the skirmish, Kate Thompson had worked a disappearing trick, her method probably as simple as passing through the door. Joshua crossed the chaos of the Magnet's big room in swift strides. This business wasn't going to be as straightforward as they'd figured.

He found the door locked. He backed off, raised his right foot and kicked hard and effectively, a short way left of the knob. The door flew open, crashing against the wall of the dim and narrow passage beyond.

Entering the passage, he saw two shapes – female figures – struggling with a bulky burden on their way to a further door which was open to the shadowy side alley between the saloon and the neighbouring hotel.

He called out. 'Hey! Hold hard there, will you?'

One girl gave a shrill cry, but neither heeded his request.

Joshua leaped down the passage and grabbed the arm of the nearest girl. It was Thompson. She said nothing at all but raked his face with her fingernails. Joshua held on and a struggle developed.

The other girl screamed and broke away from the mêlée. She went staggering out into the alley, almost drunkenly, lugging a heavy sack with her.

Joshua had his hands full with Kate; she was a spitting, scratching parcel of fury. 'Quieten down, you little wildcat!'

Behind him he heard others starting to enter the passage from the saloon.

'Bust the damn' door down he did, I tell yuh!'

'What's a-goin' on out here?'

Kate at last opened her mouth and was strident in voicing indignation that wasn't entirely a sham. 'Unhand me, mister! What d'you think you're doing? A girl says no, she means no. Let me go!'

'Why, it's the sneaky Pink!' a miner said. 'He's taken the chance to grab sweet Kate.'

Another growled with contempt, 'Set her loose, dick! Kate always says no to that stuff.'

One of the crowd pounced. 'Go take a cold bath, Dillard.' He pulled Joshua clear of the girl. It tore the shoulder of her blouse. Buttons were sent popping and lacy trim trailed adrift.

'What the–! Stay out of this, you fools,' Joshua said.

Kate ignored the exposure of flesh normally hidden from the eyes of polite society, hitched up her skirts and fled into the cinder-paved alley and the night. By the time Joshua could convince the crowd pressing into the passage that he hadn't been assaulting the dance-hall girl, she was nowhere to be seen.

'Look!' He turned their disbelieving eyes

with the one short, terse word and a jab of his finger at the open doorway to Aces Axford's office.

The evidence was there for the dumbest to see that this was maybe not so simple.

'Axford's been robbed,' Joshua said. 'My guess is the whole bloody business in the saloon was a diversion.'

Slumped just inside the office, where the girls had pushed his unconscious, skinny carcass, was Fingers O'Malley. It was the man whose appearance on the Cox City streets had bothered Joshua. His juxtaposition with the yawning emptiness of the Magnet's opened safe finally prompted Joshua's memory on his name and profession, as recorded in the Pinkerton Detective Agency's collection of mugshots.

*O'Malley, safebreaker, of New York.*

The crook had a sizeable knot on the back of his head.

Joshua told Axford, who'd joined the huddle of men at his office door, the man's suspected identity; that he was the very person he'd mentioned to him before.

'There was another girl besides Kate Thompson. I reckon the two of them were in cahoots with the saloon bandits and O'Malley,' he said. 'But they decided to double-cross the whole passel, betray 'em with that letter and take your gold for themselves.'

Axford scanned the gathering, murmuring audience with displeasure. He spotted his head barkeep and made swift, not-too-subtle dumbshow motions with his hands.

The barkeep shouted. 'Everybody back in the saloon. It's drinks on the house, gents!'

Once the crowd and a reviving but dazed safebreaker were out of his hair, Axford treated Joshua to the bluster of a man in a blazing temper, yet only too aware of his own contribution to his embarrassment.

'This is too bad, Dillard! Wye is dead and thousands of dollars of gold have been stolen. Governor Edgerton had you posted here to stop this kinda thing – and we have the biggest robbery the city has known.'

'We've Fingers O'Malley under arrest,' Joshua suggested, looking for a positive angle, knowing that Axford's accusation was grossly unfair; that everything had conspired to bring his detective work and heroic efforts to naught.

'O'Malley's penitentiary-bound, for sure, but his mouth's closed tight as a miser's purse. You heard what he said: he's not peaching on his pards, whatever happens to him. A hardened jailbird from way back.'

'I ain't exactly happy about it myself, Aces,' Joshua said. 'With some help from interferers, that girl of yours outwitted us both – probably Blackie Dukes and his gang to boot.'

Axford laughed scornfully. 'I pity anybody who tries to put one over Dukes. A right ornery cuss. And that young hell-raiser of his, Billy McGee'd know where to find her, here or at the hotel right next door.' Joshua thought he took comfort from the notion. 'A gal that made fools of the Dukes crowd wouldn't much suit 'em... wouldn't last long.'

'Yeah ... well, I guess the hotel's where I'd better be calling next, but I don't think Kate Thompson's going to be there. She was seen and recognized by folks who knew her. She'll be on the dodge. What about the other girl, the one only I saw, who got away with the loot? Did Thompson have a special friend?'

'Hannah Powell maybe,' Axford answered promptly. 'She's another of my gals. Lives in a cabin on the edge of town, out by the creek.'

'Hmm. Could be Thompson might flee there, if she ain't over to the hotel. Now if you'll pardon me, I'd better get moving, Aces. That gold can't have gotten too far yet.'

Joshua's enquiries at the hotel drew a blank. His call on Hannah Powell garnered still less. Kate Thompson wasn't 'holed up' in her cabin. Hannah had never heard of such a thing.

'Kate can come and go as she pleases, but it's my night off and she's working,' she said.

Joshua played tough. 'Quit lying, Miss Powell. What have you done with that sack of loot you hauled away from the Magnet less than an hour ago?'

She glared back at him. 'Told you, mister, I don't know nothing.' Her face was hard as rock, except for a just perceptible, nervous quiver of her chin.

'It won't wash, my lady. I saw you there.'

Hannah grabbed up the opened liquor bottle that stood on her parlour table amid the uncleared debris of an old meal. She took a generous swig.

'Mistaken identity,' she said flatly. 'You detectiving men are all the same. Full of fancy notions. And I ain't nobody's lady. Get outa here, will you?'

She deliberately and loudly belched at Joshua – a fumy one to underscore her lack of pretensions to ladyship.

Joshua pulled a sour face. 'Thank you kindly,' he said, with forced politeness. 'I guess I'd better be leaving you then.'

Relief started to creep into Hannah's stony eyes. Joshua killed it.

'But let me give you a little bit of advice:

Blackie Dukes and his crowd won't take long to figure Kate Thompson's done the dirty on them. They'll come looking here for sure, and their questioning is liable to be rougher than mine. You'll have hell to pay.'

The dove slumped into a chair at the table and propped her wobbly chin in a shaking hand. 'You don't scare me, Danford or Dillard, or whatever you want to call yourself. I ain't in no trouble in Cox City.'

'Then there isn't anything for you to worry about, is there?' Joshua said. His sarcastic tone made it obvious he was suggesting quite the reverse.

He reckoned he wouldn't find a better note on which to quit the woman's squalid home. He left with a tauntingly cheerful 'Goodnight, Miss Powell.'

Joshua's warning hadn't been designed purely to throw a scare into Hannah Powell. He laid a bet with himself that Blackie Dukes and company would come calling on her, looking for the confederate who'd double-crossed them.

The cocky kid, Billy McGee, in particular, would have had his nose put out of joint. As the member who'd probably recruited Kate Thompson, he'd not look good in the eyes of the gang. He'd need to vent his spleen on someone. From examples he'd seen of his humour, Joshua suspected a vindictive streak ran through the handsome young hell-raiser who was so full of himself.

Joshua left the cabin but shrewdly went no further than an overlooking slope grown with alder, black oak and mountain ash. He hunkered down in the brush that grew under the nearest trees' canopy and prepared to keep vigil.

But by the first light of a new day, Joshua was forced to admit to himself that his hunch hadn't worked out. Kate had not shown. Nor had any of the Dukes bunch, bent on forcing the truth out of Hannah. And Joshua was damp and cold, thirsty and hungry.

He began the trudge back to town. A small boy was throwing stones idly into the creek. Not being entirely ready to give up on his bet, he approached the ragamuffin.

'You live hereabouts, button?'

'Sure, if'n yuh call it livin',' he said with a bleak-eyed wisdom beyond his years.

'You want to do something useful, earn some money?'

The urchin was willing; Joshua promptly arranged to be contacted at the Magnet pronto if a group of men went to Hannah Powell's cabin.

Feeling a mite easier in his mind, Joshua continued into town. He found talk there monopolized by the robbery of the Magnet by one of its saloon girls and the deaths of Deputy Wye and others in a bloody gun battle.

Kate Thompson was known widely on account of her extraordinary prettiness, her singing and dancing in the Magnet's stage shows, and an alleged purity of body out of line with her occupation. Everyone conjectured on her whereabouts. Impromptu searches for her were under way.

The day wore on. The girl was not found.

She'd vanished without leaving a trace.

Meanwhile, Joshua's own name was also much bandied about – and unfairly besmirched along with the reputation of the Pinkerton Detective Agency.

Night was falling again and a crisp wind drove icy draughts through the crudely chinked cracks between the logs of Hannah Powell's cabin. It was an unwelcome reminder that winter wasn't far off.

Hannah nursed her bottle, glad of the spreading warmth it put into her stomach. Liquor made what she had left of a pitiful life tolerable. Now even her friend Kate was gone, too. The Magnet gold snatch had misfired. She herself was suspected. She daren't touch even her own share of the loot. It had been a bad mistake letting Kate put her up to stunning the New York crook.

She wondered how far Kate had fled. Was she safe now, or facing new dangers in the western Montana wilderness?

The sound of hoofbeats outside stirred her

from her alcoholic lethargy. The riders were pulling up. Oh God! She remembered Dillard's warning about the wrath of Blackie Dukes and his bunch. She drained the rest of her opened bottle in five quick swallows.

They swept into her poor sanctuary like a tornado. Dukes wrenched her up from her chair and shook her. The bone-white, sharp-featured face he thrust into hers was like an axehead. It chopped words at her. His men were all a-swirl in her blurry vision, making crashing noises as they proceeded to dismantle what there was of the mean furnishings.

'Where's your pal Kate Thompson, whore?' Dukes said.

'D-don't know nothin', you bastards,' she said, her teeth chattering, her words slurred. 'You got no right to come leapin' in my place like a pack of savages.'

Billy McGee leered over Dukes's shoulder, the charming airs the kid was wont to affect all melted away by anger. 'Don't give us no sassy lip, yuh old bag! If yuh got a lick o' sense, yuh gonna talk.'

But Hannah was insistent. She might not amount to much, but she could be loyal to the end. And there wasn't much men could do to her that she didn't know about.

'Can't say what's become of Kate,' she persevered. 'Gospel truth.'

'What did she do with the Magnet's gold then?' Dukes said, his stretched patience nudging zero. 'You were friends. You have to know something.'

'We're wastin' our time, Blackie,' one of the bunch interrupted. 'She ain't gonna answer no polite questions. Let's get on with persuadin' her proper.'

'An' how do you suggest we do that?'

An icy glitter lit Billy McGee's blue eyes. 'Take her outside and upend her in the rain barrel. If it don't drown her, it'll clear her head an' mem'ry considerable, the drunken bitch!'

A chorus of approval greeted the kid's suggestion. Despite her befuddlement, Hannah was struck with terror.

They dragged her, struggling and kicking, from the cabin. The lid was tossed off the barrel that collected runoff from the cabin's roof. Two of the bunch's biggest grabbed her arms and legs and she was suddenly up and over, her skirts around her waist and her head plunging toward the dirty water and sticky sludge collected in the barrel's bottom.

She screamed. Her mouth, nose and ears filled with the noisome contents, which she spat out as they hoisted her up again.

'Ready to spill it, whore?'

'No! No!'

The pair holding her legs lowered her head a second time. Somebody asked, 'Shall we take her drawers down?' Another said, 'Don't yuh mean *up?*'

Snickerings accompanied this show of wit.

'Naw,' said McGee. 'She's so used to barin' her ass that'd prob'ly make her feel comf'table ... like business was normal.'

More mirthless laughter was muffled as her head went under the water yet again.

And whatever the conflicting advice on her torture, all the vulnerable parts best exposed to their attention were comprehensively slapped, pinched and poked between the several subsequent duckings.

Finally, spluttering, bruised and sore from the multiple indignities – afraid for the means to earn a future livelihood and her very life – she was forced to give them something like what she thought they wanted to hear.

'Yes, yes. Kate has gold, all of it. She left Cox City last night an' won't be comin' back – ever!'

'Where's she gone?'

'I don't know... God's truth, I don't know.'

And at that, a pistol shot crashed out from the trees closest upslope from the cabin.

# 6

## KATE ON THE DODGE

With a certain satisfaction from his marksmanship, Joshua saw Billy McGee's white sombrero fly from his head. The fancy hat was holed much as the delinquent holed high-toned folks' hats himself when he was on a spree.

Weaving from point to vantage point in the brush, Joshua sent more slugs zipping round the feet of McGee's pards, setting them dancing and snatching out their own sidearms.

The hardcases, shouting angrily and waving their arms in his direction, let off a few retaliatory shots and moved quickly away from Hannah Powell and the open space between the trees and the barrel.

They rounded the cabin into its cover and headed for their mounts beyond. From the cusses and yells, it was plain they'd no idea who was coming to the whore's rescue. Or how many.

Joshua saw Hannah's legs were thrashing wildly as she strived to press her hands against the barrel's bottom and keep her head above the water. As soon as the Dukes bunch was climbing into its saddles, Joshua called to the young helper who'd run to town to fetch him. The camp urchin was accompanied by a still younger ragged brat who'd tagged along behind them.

'You kids – help Miss Powell out of the barrel!'

Joshua broke from the trees and hurtled to the corner of the cabin. Peering round it, he triggered his six-shooter twice more into the dustcloud of the escaping riders. Guns roared back, the muzzle flashes momentarily lighting the gritty fog. He ducked back and lead chewed wood from the end of a log.

By the time he looked out again, revolvers

were poor weapons for the distance. The Dukes bunch was about gone from sight – a receding tattoo of galloping hoofs, out of range.

Joshua went back round the cabin to where the two ragamuffins had tipped the barrel on to its side. Hannah was crawling out, mortified by extrication from her predicament by two wide-eyed boys, but greatly sobered by her immersion. For a while she'd feared the experience might prove fatal.

'Clean all the spongy muck outa the bottom o' your barrel fer two bits,' the older boy said, with a ready eye for making a profit.

Hannah declined the offer firmly. 'No, thank you. Put the barrel right back where it was, with the lid on. Then you can run along. Jimmy Higgins ... and not a word 'bout this to anyone, y'understand?'

Jimmy shrugged. 'Sure, ma'am. But I seen wimmin's legs afore, y'know.'

'I seen my sister with no clothes on,' piped up the smaller boy.

'Do what she says and make tracks, kids,'

Joshua said. 'I've already paid you plenty for fetching me.'

When they'd scampered away, he turned to Hannah. 'Maybe now you'll be agreeable to telling me more. I *know* you were involved, and you confessed to Dukes that you knew Kate had gone.'

The bedraggled dove swept the wet hair off her face. 'Ain't much more to tell. Mr Dillard,' she said, contrite. 'I can't show no gold to no one. I reckon Kate lit a shuck straight off – last night. She planned to ride out there and then anyway. That's everything I know.'

Joshua was thoughtful. 'Ride out? Kate was a horsewoman?'

'Yeah, she was a lot of things. A damn' fine little actress, too. I told her she should have taken to the boards; the real theatre, not throwing up her legs on a platform in a saloon. I'm gonna miss that gal...'

But Joshua was scarcely listening. He needed to pursue his enquiries elsewhere. He took his leave and hurried back into Cox

City. There he went to the livery stable. It was a dimly lit, large, smelly barn that was the boom town's second most-established business after the Magnet.

The nighthawk was lolling back in an armchair in what served as an office and harness-room, reading a Beadle dime novel. He told Joshua he hadn't been on duty the previous night.

'But I'd've heard for sure if that pretty saloon gal had come in an' bought hosses. Whole town's bin talkin' most all day 'bout nothin' else 'cept Kate Thompson bein' on the dodge with a peck o' gold.'

Joshua frowned and drummed his fingers on the counter. 'If she rode out, where else would she have gotten a mount?' he muttered to himself.

The unenthusiastic hostler chucked aside his novel, heaved himself to his feet and consulted a filthy ledger. He ran a grubby and broken-nailed finger down the page. 'Whatcha know? There was a late customer yesterday. Bought a saddle horse an' a pack-horse. Good 'uns, too, if I recall 'em c'rectly.'

'Who was this person?'

'J. Smith, it says here. Paid cash in equivalent dust. Quite normal in these parts, o' course.'

Joshua's hopes started to build. 'Where can I find last night's dutyman?'

The hostler scratched his head. 'That'd be Curtis Reisman.' He gave a dirty grin; chuckled. 'You won't be findin' *him* tonight, 'less yuh're game to go roamin' through all them whores' huts and tents on the fringe o' the diggings.' He gestured in the direction where Hannah Powell had her cabin, a dismal area generally reckoned to be Cox City's red-light district.

With 3,000 single prospectors in the Gulch, every one of the places of prostitution would at this hour be in busy operation. The task of searching them for Reisman was too ridiculous and extensive to contemplate, so more delay was enforced on Joshua before he could check the tantalizing lead held out by the barn's register. He spent the small hours sleepless and seething in his hotel room.

Even at this stage in Joshua's life, the loss of the money represented by the gold stolen from Axford's safe did not loom as his largest concern. What did, was the knowledge that his good name was unjustly being dragged in the mire. And while he tossed and turned, Kate Thompson was on the dodge somewhere, in flight, escaping further and further from the clutches of what this turbulent territory thought was justice.

Another cause for disquiet was the possible reactions to this piece of lawlessness by Governor Sidney Edgerton – sure to hear of it from his apparent friend, Aces Axford – and by his Pinkerton supervisor, Boise Flagler. Joshua had done everything humanly possible for one man, but would they know that?

Curtis Reisman turned up at the livery stable around seven after a bleak and sunless dawn. The cutting wind of the previous day was picking up and ominous dark clouds were building in the north. He ambled through the barn's main doorway and stamped his feet in the aisle between the stalls. ''Mornin', Horace,' he called out to the night man. 'Gonna be a cold 'un ... Howdy, mister, you lookin' fer me?'

Joshua was already there, waiting for him. He met a hulking man, with a stupid look on his broad face, wearing a tattered sheepskin coat over a dirty shirt and dirty Levis.

His intellect was no better than his appearance suggested, though he supplied basic information well enough.

'It were a young feller, a down-an'-out prospector type. Chuckin' it in, goin' back to the California fields, he said.'

'What did he look like?' Joshua asked.

'Black hair, kinda cropped rough ... don't 'member that much.'

'Could he have been a woman in man's duds?'

Reisman laughed scornfully. 'Didn't *feel* 'im, yuh know.'

'Was he bearded, clean-shaven?'

'Blackened cheeks and chin. Could've bin

more dirt than stubble, I guess. Had the voice of a boy, but I didn't think anythin' of it. Thar's kids of fifteen an' less in any mining camp, lyin' 'bout their ages.'

Joshua asked a few more questions, but got no helpful answers. The 'boy' had ridden out of town, heading west with a minimum of gear, and that was it.

Immediately, Joshua rented two animals for himself and set off in pursuit, if it could be called that.

The most obvious trail west from Broken Man Gulch went out over undulating country and ascended a rugged projection of the Rocky Mountains, trending north to Deer Lodge before following the twistings of the Hellgate River. The route then accessed the valley of another river, the St Regis, which led to a series of canyons and the wild and timbered heights of the Bitterroot mountain range.

Beyond lay the Coeur d'Alene Mission and open, rolling country where Joshua might gain word of his quarry at one of the numerous rude taverns, ferry shacks, lone horse camps or stage stations. Because of the Montana gold rushes, it was a well-travelled road in season.

A fugitive's destination would be Lewiston. Here a body could lose itself in a lusty, bustling centre of population where, in 1863, Sidney Edgerton had mysteriously failed to report for swearing-in as Chief Justice of Idaho Territory.

The whole trip on horseback would take some two weeks. Kate Thompson had a day and a half's start on Joshua. But he reckoned he might be able to make it up and catch her.

Plucky Kate Thompson was not in the victorious frame of mind that Joshua Dillard imagined.

For a start, she was toting no half a sack of gold. That part of her plan had been thwarted by the intervention of the alleged Pinkerton detective. Once she'd been caught in the act of robbery, and the hunt for her was on, she'd been forced to quit Cox City with just one pouch of gold she'd thankfully shoved into the waistband of her skirt while still at the Magnet. She'd not dared to visit her accomplice's cabin, but had fled forthwith to her hotel room to don her prepared disguise and proceed straight away to make good her escape.

So much for riches and a fresh start in life! The panic had gone very hard against her grain.

The second disaster was the weather. The first heavy snow of winter began falling early – two days into her brave journey to Lewiston. The snow was light at first and, since the wind had dropped, the flakes alighted on her soft as feathers, and spread tree and rock with a clean white mantle, pleasing to behold. But then the flakes grew larger and heavier; fleecier.

The north wind picked up again. Snow swirls became flurries. A low moaning succeeded the muffling, peaceful silence of the first fall. An anxious frown creased Kate's brow. Soon, a real blizzard swept down the deserted trail. Fresh-fallen snow was swept into drifts that filled the troughs in the road, making the going difficult for her horses.

The wind penetrated Kate's clothing, each gust like a knife thrust into her shivering flesh. Its song rose to a high, shrill whistle. Her horses lowered their heads. The snowflakes became icy chips that stung Kate's face like it was being worked on with pointed needles to produce some gruesome tattoo.

To bring some warmth to her body and restore circulation to her numbed extremities, Kate dismounted and stamped her feet and slapped her arms about her body. She had a horror of disfiguring frostbite. Haunting pictures came to mind of lost fingers and toes and never being able to dance again.

Her face became stiff and frozen. She rubbed soft snow over the delicate skin to protect her nose and ears in particular. Walking beside the stumbling horses for a few miles, she soon became short of breath. The mountain air was thin and she grew light-headed; each step a struggle in the face of the wind and the driving ice-storm.

At what she thought was every half-hour, Kate rested a few minutes to catch her breath and rub her hands, face and ears with more snow. Darkness fell and she lost all track of time. But she dared not stop, despite a powerful longing for sleep. She knew that if she were to lie down in an alluring, soft bed of snow in some relatively sheltered bottom of a timbered mountain pass, she'd suffocate.

The road, as she remembered it, should by now have brought her to the settlement at Deer Lodge. She began to panic, like she had on the night of the robbery – an unpleasant sensation that churned her insides.

What if she'd lost her sense of direction in the snowstorm and deviated from her route? The snow had sometimes been thick as milk and the ground had disappeared under a blanket of white. What if she was maybe wandering in a circle?

To keep up her spirits and to keep awake,

she began to sing to herself. Not the songs she'd sung in the saloons, but old folk airs and hymns she'd learned as a small child before she was orphaned.

# 7

## 'LET ME HIDE MYSELF...'

It was shortly before what should have been sundown. Joshua, well prepared, equipped and provisioned, was making good progress on the north-westerly leg of his lonely chase after Kate. Since at times he'd been riding into the teeth of a howling blizzard, he wasn't displeased.

In fact, his chief worries revolved around the safety and well-being of the winsome saloon girl he'd watched in Cox City. She'd displayed remarkable, unexpected resource-fulness, but he had to wonder how she was faring in the exceptionally bleak weather. It might take her more than spunkiness to survive.

The first sign that there might be other human life ahead of him in the stark wilderness was a glimmer of light through the haze of falling snow.

The second sign was something else.

The full fury of the storm had passed and, above its low and mournful wail across the white uplands, he heard another, human song. It was mournful, plaintive, eerie ... yet somehow unbelievably beautiful. It sent a different kind of chill down his spine.

*'Rock of Ages, cleft for me,*
*Let me hide myself in Thee...'*

His approach obscured by gentle snow, his horses' hoof-falls deadened, he came upon Kate Thompson in the lee of a timbered ridge that provided a windbreak and a degree of shelter, augmented by the up-sticking roots of a large deadfall. The toppled tree had also supplied fuel for her campfire, which was the gleam he'd seen in the greyness from afar.

Startled, the girl broke off singing and jumped to her feet. Snow fell from her bulky men's clothes into the fire; it hissed and sent up a shower of sparks.

Joshua unwound his thick wool muffler. 'Good evening. It is Miss Thompson, isn't it?' She was barely recognizable with her short-cut hair and dirt-streaked face. 'I can't say much for your choice of a campsite.'

'Mr Dillard! Have you come to take me back?'

'That's exactly what I intend. You – and all that gold you stole.'

'I haven't got the gold,' she said quickly. She brushed away a big flake of snow that had landed on her not-very-masculine nose. 'It – it's lost. You can search me if you like. I had to leave it, and now I'm lost, too.'

'Hidden it somewhere, no doubt,' Joshua accused drily. 'And how come you're here?'

'I think I must have turned back on myself

in the storm. Now my pack mare has gone lame and we can get no further.'

Joshua nodded and dismounted. He went to where her two horses stood under the overhang of the deadfall's roots. Kate followed him, looking downcast. He took off a glove and lifted the mare's right foreleg. The lower leg was grossly swollen.

'The tendon's damaged. How did that happen?'

'We went off the trail and stumbled into a drift. I think she must have struck a big rock under the snow.'

It was a nasty impact injury. 'Hmm!' Joshua responded, not impressed with Kate's folly. 'We'll have to rest up someplace, wait for the weather to clear and go back when best we can.'

'But I don't want to go back!' Kate cried vehemently.

Joshua laughed. 'You've no choice in the matter. I'm going to clear up the business in Cox City. Moreover, you should be glad to see me – bearings lost in a winter landscape such as this, and a horse lamed.'

'Oh, I am glad of your assistance, Mr Dillard, I don't deny that.'

'Then put out that fire and come along. I saw an abandoned logging camp not more'n a mile back and it's better cover than what you have here.' He gestured at the earthy ledge above them, and her pathetic bundle of blankets.

Kate seemed resigned to co-operating with him, but it took the best part of an hour to reach the old buildings Joshua had marked earlier. The pack mare was not especially distressed, but her gait was uneven and very slow.

The logging camp, though surrounded by a plentiful supply of raw material in the dismally dark pines, had not proved a viable venture. It was too far from the markets for its product to compete with similar operations better situated. The sawmill had been demolished and other buildings had partly collapsed. The ruins were covered by deep snow-drifts.

Joshua set them up in the bunkhouse, which still had a sound roof. An old stable was not in as good repair, but was adequate for the four horses. Night was falling; the temperature with it.

'Will the horses be all right?' Kate asked.

Joshua was able to reassure her. 'If you give 'em a choice between standing outside or inside at any given moment, you'll find most will stand outside, even in rain or snow. Their systems begin to work as nature intended, and they live healthier, happier and longer.'

'I suppose I might have known that,' she admitted. 'I've just gotten used to seeing them in stalls at the livery barn.'

Joshua shook his head and tutted. 'Foul weather probably does them less harm. The best horse doctors say that when a horse is kept in a stall, even for brief periods, it becomes over-stressed, leading to all kinds of health problems.'

'That's sad,' Kate said. 'Why, it's unfair, like – like putting a person in a prison cell. I think it's morally wrong to make horses stand in stalls day in and day out with no real reason to live. They can't be sociable through stall walls!'

Joshua was touched by her solicitude for the animals, but later he was to find her interest in them in fact had a somewhat different focus.

He had again underestimated her. He thought she'd learned a lesson about wilderness travel and was resigned to facing the consequences of her actions in Cox City. Lulled into confidence by her meek attitude, and being a gentleman, he allowed her to roll up in her blankets for the night, free and in every way unfettered, at the far end of the bunkhouse from himself.

In the morning, he found his prisoner gone. And that wasn't all: Kate Thompson had absconded with the two best horses, all the best equipment, and the lion's share of his grub and the sacks of grain that were the horses' feed.

As the sun rose on a glittering white and

empty landscape, Joshua cursed himself roundly for having put any trust in her. 'Hell! She's hightailed it – gotten clean away.'

He hated to think what Boss Flagler would say, should he hear just the straight of it... 'What! An agent of ours let a slip of a dance-hall gal pull the wool over his eyes? It's the damnedest fool thing I ever heard of!'

Again, Joshua set off in pursuit. Though it remained about time for winter to close in with a vengeance, the weather had momentarily improved. Unfortunately, Joshua reckoned this might be of greater help to Kate. He was lumbered with a part-lame pack animal that slowed his progress to barely a half-pace.

At Deer Lodge, no one would trade him a sound beast for the injured one. So they limped on to a horse camp someplace beyond the Hellgate River, in a mountain valley bordered by high hills. Here, the owner took pity on the pack mare and granted Joshua a trailworthy substitute.

Ten days later, after an arduous ride over

the Bitterroots, he arrived in Lewiston. He learned that a very similar 'young man' to the one he sought had been seen in town several days earlier. By all reports, the lad had also made the gruelling trek over the mountain passes. He'd sold up his two tired horses and was last observed boarding a Snake River paddle-steamer bound for Portland, Oregon...

No way would he be able to find Kate Thompson lone-handed now. Nor did he think the wide-flung tentacles of the Pinkerton Agency would be able to locate her. Thousands of her kind were to be found throughout the West, making their way under this name or that to ever-deeper degradation.

The dance-hall girl, like Kate's friend Hannah, was not a romantic figure. Often a forced life of debauchery would end in early death, sometimes at her own hand. Wholesale trafficking in female human flesh during these frontier days was more horrible than the atrocities committed by the wildest Indians.

Somehow, Joshua couldn't bring himself to deny Kate her chance to improve her lot in life. What was gold after all? Just something out of God's earth that men took and used as money. Viewed that way, her escape didn't matter.

On his return to Cox City, Joshua was less inclined to feel altruistic. The whole affair was over, but not over – it never would be for him personally until he knew exactly what had really happened in Broken Man Gulch, and until the lawless element, as represented almost openly by Blackie Dukes, Billy McGee and others of their stripe, were made to face justice.

He'd also like to know, if not Kate's whereabouts, then at least the resting place of the more than $35,000 in gold that had been in Aces Axford's safe.

Yet it seemed Joshua was to be denied an ending. At least for now. Axford passed him a letter, sent care of the Magnet from Boss Flagler. Joshua read it and flung it down on

Axford's mahogany desktop in disgust.

'Recalled!' he said, angry in his disappointment.

'Yeah. I know,' said Axford. 'Help yourself to a drink – a big one. It doesn't look like you're gonna have the chance to wrap this one up, Joshua my boy.'

'What's it all about, Aces?'

'Far as I can figure, Governor Edgerton is about to quit. He's a rich man and wants to head back to his old home in Ohio. He ain't interested any more in Cox City bandits.'

'That was in the wind from the start,' Joshua said, with the passion of one betrayed.

'I'm a square-shooter, Joshua, as you know. I doubt Edgerton's enthusiasm for a Pinkerton solution here was stoked any when you let the Magnet gold get stolen from under our noses.' Axford waved his cheroot to encompass the smoke-blue air around his head. 'The whole territory heard about that.'

It was now generally known that because the gold-rush town had no bank, he had agreed to give successful miners space in his safe to store their wealth – at their own risk, of course.

Joshua let Axford's swipe lie. It was far from the truth. No one faced with similar circumstances could have done better. His detective work had been impeccable. He'd acted decisively, but been undermined by Deputy Wye and ignorant citizens. His only fault had been in showing his captive a gallant solicitude.

He swore that one day he'd redeem himself in Montana.

Within weeks, Joshua was back to checking on illegal horse racing, in which the underworld was very active. Agents were detailed to check on the certification of every track across America, and the people behind the grandstands.

The Pinkerton strategy was to expand a network of ever-watchful man-hunters that could close in, like a noose, on the nation's villains, east and west. The tactics were a taunting harassment. The agency made dangerous enemies for its operatives.

This Joshua found out the hard way as one year succeeded another. At first, his heart's total desire was for a living spiced with adventure and excitement, and the satisfaction of jobs well done. But a bright-eyed, peachy-cheeked young lady made counter-claims on his heart and he took her for a wife.

Then he learned that thief-taking and wife-taking didn't mix. One day of sickening bloodshed in San Antonio, Texas, 'Pink'-haters came calling, wrecking the Dillard home, snuffing out the warming flame that was his beautiful young wife's life.

Joshua's own life and nature were irrevocably changed. His heart turned to stone. He became reckless, hating all lawbreakers with what was rightly called obsession. Variously, stories had it he resigned from the agency, or was sacked. Perforce, he became a free agent, a drifter growing lean and very hard from an assortment of shrewdly chosen assignments. Most of these ended in blood and turmoil, none quite his own death, and all with very little monetary reward to show for what he achieved.

He almost forgot about the Cox City affair.

But seven years after he'd last been in the place, and when he was at the bottom of his financial barrel, he received an offer from its town council. His reputation as a gun-handy, freelance trouble shooter had spread and the council was inviting him to become Cox City's marshal and clean up 'some lawlessness'.

The money tempted him. It was $200 a month plus fines collected. Yet more than this was the thought of at last regaining esteem in that country.

It was high time, Joshua thought, for unfinished business to be taken up. On receipt of the council's letter, he committed himself there and then to making good on the old promise sworn to himself in Aces Axford's office.

# 8

## LILLY HONEYDEW

In a coulée several miles out of Cox City, Blackie Dukes and his bunch sat their horses wearing dusters and neckpieces pulled up over their faces. They'd graduated from small-time muggers of prospectors to big-time road agents. They waited behind cover alongside the stage road to jump the coach from Bannack.

Listening for the distant rattle and rumble of the approaching Concord on the bumpy road, Billy McGee asked Dukes, 'Think they'll try an' fight their way through?'

'Could be. I do hear tell the new smart-ass town marshal is taking a strong line, urging the stage company to hire on tougher guards.'

McGee scowled and grumbled under his neckpiece. 'Hell, ain't Cox City's new peace officer that ex-Pinkerton dick we ran rings around way back? Can't think why the ol' coots on the council wanted him.'

'Seems like he's gotten a diff'rent rep since then, Billy,' Dukes sneered. 'Hard man, quick on the trigger.'

'Well, I sure did never hear of Joshua Dillard as no town-tamer, that's a fact. No great respecter o' the law hisself, they do say. Kinda bounty man.'

Another hardcase said, 'It's a wise plan not to believe half what you hear in that thar fancy Magnet, Billy.'

'Aw, drop it, boys, this ain't time for quarrelling and bickering,' Dukes said. 'Remember – outa city jurisdiction we still gotten a neck-hold on the sheriff, so Dillard ain't momentarily our partic'lar concern.'

The coach was coming at breakneck speed. It could be heard at considerable distance across the sun-baked, broken land. The sounds of its progress built and waned in the hot stillness as it slammed into coulées, laboured out of them, ran on and dropped again. Soon, the coach would plunge into the bottom where the road agents waited and the dirt road curved past the massive rock towering a hundred feet above them, giving shade and cover.

When the coach came into sight, the driver applied the brake and slackened the speed of the team into the dip, the safer to negotiate the curve. The masked riders swarmed out and surrounded the slowing rig.

Dukes yelled above its racketing passage, 'Pull in, Jehu!' And seeing the guard reach down for the rifle lying along the footboard by their boots, added, 'Don't touch that gun, mister!'

But the guard was foolhardy and had his orders from company bosses. He flipped the Winchester to his shoulder. 'Feed the team leather, driver!' he snapped. 'Cox City's straight ahead – no more'n minutes' runn–'

Riding abreast of the careering coach, Dukes levelled his Colt and triggered. The

.45-calibre bullet ended the guard's advice and his life instantly. It hurtled through his skull – skin, bone, brain, everything in its all-destructive path. Blood and tissue spattered from a gory exit hole over his stage-driver companion.

The shocked driver shouldered the corpse off him and it toppled from the seat, thumping along the side of the stage, inscribing an arc of red on the glossy black paintwork before it thudded into the dust. Another bullet winged past the driver's shoulder.

'Ain't sense in both getting killed,' Dukes shouted. 'You play peaceable and you won't lose anything but money.'

The driver applied the brake, stood up and hauled on the reins. He roared at his horses. The coach's locked wheels skidded and made long tracks in the hot dust. Standstill was reached in a choking, buff cloud, the horses blowing from their run and shaking slobber from their chins.

'We want the strongboxes headed for the Cox City bank,' Dukes told the trembling driver. 'Both! The one under your seat an' the one at the back.'

While the driver lugged out the nearer box, two of the outlaws dismounted and slashed the black, oiled-leather cover off the rack at the rear of the coach.

Billy McGee slid from his saddle and picked up the rifle dropped by the guard. He went to the coach, looked in with eyes still adjusted to the harsh sunlight and saw the shapes of three cowering passengers.

'Ever'body out with hands high!' He pointed the rifle into the shadowy interior. 'Jump to it!'

Behind him, gunshots busted the locks of the strongboxes.

The trio in the stage started to pile out. The first man was an obvious drummer type, with shiny patches on his coat and pants, clutching a portmanteau, probably filled with samples, and looking mournfully resigned. Maybe this had happened to him before.

'There's a lady in there, feller,' he said, as though accusing McGee of an impropriety.

'No diff'rence,' McGee drawled, enjoying the bullying. 'She steps out if'n she's the Queen o' Sheba.'

But the next to emerge was another man, who turned to help the woman clamber down. The man, who had a silver-headed cane tucked under his arm, was a swarthy Latin type – somehow not Mexican – with a disparaging smirk on his loose-lipped, clean-shaven face.

The woman was tall, graceful and slender, but with a fullness in what McGee regarded as highly important places. She had a ridiculous hat set atop a pile of blonde hair and three strands of pearls about her neck.

'Well, well...' McGee said, in a voice that had to accompany a leer on his hidden face, 'what have we here?'

He might well have asked, for it was difficult to make out anything informative from the woman's countenance, which was so liberally daubed with powder and paint as to look like a mask. Only once could McGee remember having seen females more heavily done up – and those were members of a touring opera company.

'Damn it,' the man replied, 'this lady is Miss Lilly Honeydew, the celebrated songstress, straight from a sellout season in Sacramento. You can't get away with your insolence.'

McGee laughed. 'Shuck yuhself of any guns an' your valuables, mister – rings, watches, money an' such. You, too, drummer. An' the handsome lady can take off her pearls.'

'Fool!' exploded the swarthy type. 'They're stage stuff; paste, counterfeit. All my wife's jewellery is imitation.'

'Yuh mean fake? An' *Miss* Honeydew's your woman?'

'My wife, scum. The lady's professional name is Miss Honeydew, but she's Mrs Ramon Betzinez and I am her husband and manager.'

'A fake maiden, too, huh?' McGee taunted. 'Mebbe we boys better hold on to her an' study on these things…'

'Leave it, kid,' Dukes ordered. 'We ain't got time for tomfoolery. Collect their valuables, then let's have them lying face down on the ground beside the driver.'

The drummer meekly handed over a watch and chain together with the bills from a greasy leather wallet. He had no arms.

But the singer's manager said to his wife, 'Give him nothing, Lilly. I'll certainly not.'

'He'll shoot you, Ramon,' the woman said, though McGee thought rather matter-of-factly, without the emotion expected from a loving wife.

McGee reversed the rifle in his hands and slammed its barrel against the side of Betzinez's head.

'Think again, yuh pimp!'

Blood oozing from a torn ear, Betzinez sullenly complied and gave the outlaws his money, rings and a gold watch from his vest pocket. And he lay face down alongside the drummer. 'They'll pay for this, you can depend on it,' he muttered to his fellow traveller.

McGee thought about adding the silver-headed cane to the robbery's smaller pickings, but thought better of it. It looked kind of cumbersome, so he let it lie in the dust. He strode up to Lilly Honeydew, glared into her eyes and twisted his fist into the strings of pearls at her throat.

Despite his powerful tug, the woman stood her ground and her eyes returned his glare, unflinching. The strands broke and several of the allegedly bogus pearls escaped his clutch and bounced on the rocky roadway. He shoved the rest into a pocket of his duster.

Something he'd seen, maybe in her eyes, gave McGee pause. Behind him, Dukes said, 'Mount up, kid – the money's in our gunny sacks an' we're outa here.'

Irritated by the thing he couldn't quite put his finger on, McGee shifted the rifle into the crook of his arm and took his bowie from his belt left-handed. He'd work off his frustration inflicting some indignity she couldn't ignore.

He hooked the knifepoint through the

neckband of Lilly Honeydew's bodice and pulled outward. The brocade ripped; with a second deft flick, laces beneath were snagged and cut by the blade.

The bowie was wickedly sharp, ten inches long, sharpened only on one side to the curve of the tip, then sharpened on both sides to the point. A cunningly designed handguard of brass permitted McGee to slide his hand down over the blade as necessary and gave him perfect control of it as both a fighting weapon and a versatile tool.

The woman's neck and the upper portion of her bosom were suddenly revealed. Drawn forward, gasping at last in horrified fear of what he might do next with the knife, she stumbled and fell on to her knees.

But the sight of her *décolletage* displayed like a common saloon girl's didn't alleviate McGee's bother as he'd intended. Oddly, it was deepened.

'C'mon, you jackass!' Dukes rapped. 'The party's over.'

McGee quit his unsatisfying sport and

flung himself into his saddle. The gang made off at a hard run.

It was some minutes before the stage-driver made bold enough to get back on his feet. Not much was said, but with the aid of the two male passengers the guard's bloody and broken corpse was lashed on to the stage's rear rack and decently covered.

The driver climbed back on the box. The man who'd shared his high seat was dead, he was minus the most significant part of his cargo and a usable Colt revolver, and his three passengers were robbed and battered.

He kicked off the brake, took hold of the lines and set the team in motion. 'Giddup!' he called. 'Get the hell outa here!' The coach rolled on toward Cox City.

In the dust, a spilled pearl was left to glisten in the sun-scorched silence like a teardrop.

Cox City was a boom-town that had survived. Many of the mining camps became ghost towns inside of a decade. This wasn't one of them. Diversification had worked its wonders. To the immediate south and east was a stretch of country dotted with small ranches. A little further afield was a prosperous patch of cattle country with herds brought up from Texas.

The sands of Broken Man Gulch had yielded tens of millions of dollars in gold dust in their time, but the placers had mostly played out. Cox City had managed to stay alive as a business centre serving the nearby mining and ranching areas.

At the town's heart, the mixed economy had produced five handsome brick blocks, no fewer than six general stores, three hotels, three livery barns, a bank and a newspaper office. A stone courthouse was under construction; a six-company army post was only four miles away.

But the circumstances overall were not so much different as developed. It was still largely a masculine world with some rough edges most evident in the town's seven saloons. Similarly, Joshua Dillard found that pre-eminent among these venues was the Magnet. Aces Axford, flashy as ever, had tried very hard to deliver on his old brag that he'd elevate the Magnet into the fanciest spot in Montana.

The place sparkled with gilt and glitter. The promised chandeliers and the paintings of the voluptuous nudes hung in the appropriate positions. A roulette wheel span on gears said by disgruntled losers to be rigged – but only out of earshot of the burly bouncers.

The Magnet, as before, was thronged with drinkers and a crew of barkeepers was constantly on the move, perspiring in the thick, smoky atmosphere. The gambling layouts continued to do big business and the dance floor was packed with townsmen, ranch-hands and miners tripping over the daintier feet of the establishment's provocatively garbed ladies – hostesses in low-cut formal gowns and short-skirted house girls.

Joshua wondered how much of Axford's success came down to his integrity and business ability, or whether it was a classic case of having been in the right place at the right time. Whatever, the saloon-man had clung tenaciously to the initial advantage and exploited his political connections.

Axford was, by his own report, 'a good friend' of Mayor Clem Miller and his council. Nothing really changed! He was also still smoking cheroots that Joshua frankly thought foul-stinking. He blew a smoke-ring and watched it till it broke and dispersed.

'I must confess, Joshua, I rather thought we wouldn't have the pleasure of seeing you in these parts again, or any more of your detectiving work,' he said. 'Yet here you are having pinned on the Cox City marshal's badge. You've become a strange one, you know that?'

Joshua moved to the window of Axford's office and took a deep breath of fresher air. 'Folks have told me the like. Your friend the mayor thought he'd be putting a fox in charge of the chicken coop by hiring me – that his council's notion was a clever one.'

'And isn't it? You've surely built a rep as a hardnosed, gunfighting man.'

'I'm good with a gun, but that don't make me a gun for hire, which is something else.'

Joshua paused to reflect silently. Personally, he saw no new issues to be resolved in Cox City, just a continuation of the ones of seven years ago with the same people involved. His new tin badge was an aid to settling them; recovering integrity. In between had been the years of drifting, the jobs done for little or no reward, and the fiery bitterness of good things in his life that had been destroyed by rogues and blackguards. He hated lawless scum with an intensity no judicial authority could accommodate.

He added, 'Well ... maybe the gun is for hire when the cause is right.'

Axford said, 'The town really needs your services, you know. The old, early crudeness lingers on, while the place is set to evolve into respectability. A multitude of ordinances need enforcing to speed the programme. Wives, mothers and sweethearts have joined the menfolk now. Robbery, rowdiness, public nuisances ... these things must be controlled.'

He tapped ash into the West's biggest glass ashtray.

'Our inhabitants long to imitate the culture and refinements of Eastern townships,' he went on. 'After all, we exist to provide services and entertainment – especially at the Magnet.'

''Deed you do,' Joshua scoffed. Axford's joint was surely out front as the biggest, most garish in town. 'But there ain't much culture and refinement in faro, dice or hurdy-gurdy girls.'

Axford took affront, or pretended to.

'You're behind the times, Marshal,' he said stiffly. 'We still have those things, sure, but since you were here last, the Magnet has broadened its appeal. Why, just this week the acclaimed soprano Lilly Honeydew begins a season on my stage. She received rave notices in San Francisco and Sacramento.'

'Don't know 'bout that,' Joshua said with a shrug. 'But I do hear tell she was most distressed when her afternoon stage was held up by road agents.'

Axford nodded. 'Exactly. It's past time we had some tough law around here. What are you going to do about it?'

'Nothing,' Joshua said crisply. 'My jurisdiction ends at town limits. The county abides with lawlessness just as ever.'

Arford harrumphed and shaped up his waxed moustache between thumb and forefinger. 'Rumour has it the said road agents are the same hellers who remain back of much of the wildness in Cox City – Blackie Dukes and his crowd.'

'Ah, but I was informed Dukes is a respectable gent now. Ostensibly ranching.'

'True. Specially the "ostensibly". You should look into it. Make more sense than coming here with your search warrants to look for loaded dice and decks of marked cards.'

Joshua grinned. 'You know that's routine, Aces. Has to be done every month or so by all good town marshals. When a gambler with a grudge files a complaint he's been cheated in a gaming house, the peace officer has to look the place over for tricks.'

He could have added, 'But you expect it and, being smart, never leave anything around for us to find.' He got up to leave.

'Oh, yeah,' Axford confirmed, 'I appreciate that. But it'd be good to pin something on Dukes. You failed before when we suspicioned he was behind the big gold robbery from my safe. Be good to do it now, wouldn't it?'

Joshua paused in the doorway on his way out. It was pointless to explain to this hardheaded businessman that the only sense in which he'd 'failed' was in choosing not to act meanly against a cold and frightened girl, who had probably been more sinned against than sinning, and that he'd then had the rug pulled from under his feet by Governor Edgerton.

He said bleakly, 'It would.'

# 9

## THE MAGNET
## ATTRACTS TROUBLE

The saloon was crowded and living up to its name as never before. The Magnet was a cauldron of tobacco smoke, liquor fumes, ripe body odour and noise when Joshua joined the crush to see Lilly Honeydew's nightly performance. Along with her glorious crown of full blonde hair and her shapely body, set off by a green taffeta gown, Lilly's songbird talents had made her the current sensation of Cox City.

Joshua had to admit – her visual appeal notwithstanding – the beautiful renditions of the blackly sentimental 'Barbara Allen' and the lover's lament of 'Green Grow the Lilacs' were such to make the hardened roisterer sob into his tipple.

*Green grow the lilacs all sparkling with dew*
*I'm lonely, my darling, since parting with you*
*But by our next meeting I hope to prove true*
*And change the green lilacs to the red, white*
  *and blue.*

The Magnet audience was captivated by her pure soprano voice. Lilly treated them next to a version of 'Joe Bowers', a tale in song especially popular with the folks of Cox City.

Joe's story was about leaving his home and Sally Black, the girl he loved in Pike County, Missouri, to find a fortune in the California goldfields. He worked hard and saved his gold for his love. But alas, his Sally proved false. Dear brother Ike wrote to tell Joe she'd married a butcher with red hair.

It was a situation with which many of her audience could painfully identify.

Joshua noticed among the entranced crowd an old, familiar face, It was Billy

McGee's, as intent as any of them on the star attraction. Maybe more intent than any...

No doubt like his mentor Blackie Dukes, the grown-up kid was still raising hell, but with a cunning honed by each new ruckus that had erupted. Certainly, the seemingly gutless folks of Cox City remained too scared to speak up and denounce Dukes and his boys for major crimes or lesser mayhem. That was something they expected Joshua to do. And given the chance he'd take pleasure in obliging them. Nothing would satisfy him more than to get the whole ugly gang in the cells above the partly completed courthouse.

As Lilly completed the sorrowful saga of the cheated miner, Billy turned from the stage, shook his head as though in perplexity and slapped coins on the bar counter for his next drink.

Joshua thought his behaviour a mite odd. The young hardcase was no softie. He had a hunch his reaction must signify something of a different importance. Billy McGee would bear watching.

Lilly's repertoire was astonishingly wide. It included adaptations of old ballads and popular songs of English, Irish and Scottish origin. This ultimately had an unfortunate consequence, for many of these traditional tunes had acquired alternate, bawdy lyrics from the American cowboys who sang them to themselves and sleeping longhorns in wide open spaces.

The packed assembly in the Magnet contained a contingent in town from an outlying cattle outfit on a Saturday-night spree. Well liquored-up, some of the crew began joining in Lilly's refrains with obscene words of their own.

Pandemonium broke out. Shouts of censure were opposed by a competing roar of approval.

'Shame!'

'More! What about the one where Sweet Sue gets–?'

'You dirty-mouthed rats!'

'You prissy-mouthed bastards!'

A beer jug was thrown and went in the

direction of the stage. Joe 'Jingles' Wrightson lost his nerve at the keyboard, played some wrong, tinkling notes, which few heard, then upped and fled, leaving Lilly in confusion, without piano accompaniment.

Ramon Betzinez, the singer's possessive husband and agent, came striding on to the stage from the curtained wings, handsomely attired in a long-tailed black coat, striped pants, a white, ruffle-fronted shirt and a black tie. He took hold of Lilly's wrist and made as though to lead her off.

But Lilly appeared reluctant to go with him. Maybe she thought the situation could be retrieved.

Joshua couldn't hear what Betzinez said to her above the conflicting howls of cowboys and townsmen.

On the floor, a full-scale set-to was threatening, stirred along by the more usual troublemakers, the Dukes bunch rowdies. Somewhere in the direction of the bar a stack of glassware toppled with a crash. Overhead, the chandeliers chinked as they reverberated in the bedlam.

Aces Axford appeared at Joshua's side. 'You're wearing the badge, my friend. Aren't you going to do something?'

'Like what?'

'Don't town-tamers "buffalo" rioters?'

'If you mean hit 'em with the butt of a gun, you need something like a Greener for that, not a six-gun. And the tactic only works one-to-one, not for a lone man going up against a half-hundred. Where are your bouncers?'

On stage, Betzinez raised both hands – one open and the other clenching his silver-topped cane – in a mute appeal for silence. It was granted, partly.

'Listen, gentlemen! We don't like to spoil your fun, but Miss Honeydew cannot continue unless y'all settle down–'

'Like good little boys,' a Dukes wag put in. He was a fair mimic, and he parodied Betzinez's mellifluous voice, making it sound smarmier and more patronizing than it was.

The drunken cowboys cracked up again.

They whooped, hollered, slapped each others' backs and stamped their feet.

'Git back t' school, Hank!'

'L'arn yore manners, Chuck!'

Betzinez rose to the challenge – or the bait. As soon as the hullabaloo faded in intensity, he shouted, 'I'm not a schoolteacher, you filthy, uncouth cow-nurses! I'm a man of birth and breeding.'

'You talk awful big, smartypants,' an offended rangeman retorted.

'I've been talking big and acting smart most of my life. It's why I can book my client, Miss Honeydew, into the finest rooms in the land, of which this clearly is not one.'

The cowboys made derisive sounds of pretended shock at his verdict on Aces Axford's grand establishment.

'Your Miss Honeyquim sings a purty song, mister,' one of the clearer-headed said, sarcastically perverting her name. 'But we don't like your greaser face an' rubbery lips. Or your fancy speechifying. Why don't yuh light a shuck an' let us look after the li'l lady?'

His suggestion was rewarded with more noisy acclamation.

Betzinez again seized his wife's wrist, this time in what was to Joshua an obviously cruel grip, and virtually dragged her from the scene of her unevenly appreciated endeavours.

But one cowboy had put away enough whiskey for this act of passive provocation to turn him mean, mad and murderous.

'Bring our s-songbird back,' he slurred. 'Or we'll t-tear the dump to the groun'!'

One of Axford's burly bouncers finally made a play. He moved in on him, shouldering his way through a press of sweaty bodies. 'All right, feller, there'll be an end to this yellin' an' a-carryin' on. You're out!'

'By God – don' go till 'm good 'n' ready!' the drunken ranny bawled, squinting at the bouncer through bloodshot eyes.

To the horror of Joshua and the crowd, he dragged out a revolver and waved it clumsily in front of him, seeking to bring it level. Like the Red Sea dividing for the children of

Israel, a space miraculously opened up around him as parties of all persuasions in the quarrel, including the bouncer, backed away from the gun's wavering muzzle.

Damnit! Joshua thought. If the crazy galoot goes to triggering, someone here's likely to get killed. Looks like the marshal has to act, or the Dillard name'll be mud in Cox City again.

Joshua went forward boldly into the space. 'I'm the town's law,' he said, tapping his badge. 'And the law says you go now. If they've got a lick of sense, some of your friends here can help your tangled feet make it through the batwings – pronto.'

But not one of the other cowpokes made a move. A deathly stillness took hold of everybody; a sudden hush that near crackled with tension, as if before a thunderstorm.

The drunk regarded him with a cocky sneer, abruptly possessed of the shrewd wisdom of only the deeply intoxicated.

'I heared 'bout you – Dill-somep'n. Yuh ain't no real lawman. No better 'n a saddle-bum ridin' the grub line. Came in here ... horse, rig, roll back of your cantle, duds on your back ... mebbe a few spare dollars. Yuh don' scare me none, bogeyman. Shove off!'

He emphasized his order with a further erratic wave of his Colt. His finger was beginning to whiten as it tightened around the trigger.

Joshua shrugged his broad shoulders. 'Quite a passel of name-calling for a drunk.'

He turned as though he was backing down. But it was no more than pretence, a tactic designed to put the dangerous drunk off his guard.

Just as the man was opening his mouth to crow at his victory, Joshua pivoted on his heel. Few of the onlookers saw from where the Peacemaker came. The gun leapt into his right hand swift as a blinding flash of lightning. In the same, missed split-second of time, the weapon crashed.

Flame spat from its blue-black steel. The drunk was hit in his gun arm – his elbow shattered by the .45 slug. He shrieked like an injured wild animal. His gun soared from his nerveless fingers.

A new hubbub of excitement started to swell from the startled crowd. Some of the cowboys were outraged and began to edge forward, snarling.

But Joshua was standing his ground. His blue eyes glittered like ice and he swung the new Peacemaker's muzzle in an arc that covered each of the group in rapid turn.

'Anyone else who draws dies!' Joshua said decisively. 'Savvy? Next hellion to lift a gun, so help me, I shoot to kill.'

'Yuh busted Wilf Ballinger's arm!' a cowpoke protested.

Aces Axford intervened. 'He asked for it, boy. I want no killings in the Magnet.'

He turned to another of the cowmen. 'You, Dawson – you're the Double T's top-hand, ain't you? Get Ballinger and the rest of your outfit outa here.'

'Jesus, Aces ... Wilf's bin shot.' Anger deepened the colour in Dawson's liquor-flushed face. 'This greenhorn lawdog had 'no right!'

'The marshal had every right,' Axford contradicted. 'Ballinger drew a gun first. He was drunk. People were apt to get hurt or killed. Dillard acted to protect them.'

'This is so,' Joshua said. 'Do as Mr Axford suggests. If you want to make trouble, take yourself and your crew someplace else. You ain't making it in Cox City.'

If he was to have a future in the chancy business of troubleshooting, Joshua couldn't afford for matters to go wrong here. Because of what had happened seven years before – the unforgotten robbery of $35,000 in gold – Axford, Mayor Miller and the town council would lay the blame for any calamity on him; he'd no doubt whatsoever about that.

It could be because they knew he'd be aware of this that they'd taken the gamble of pinning a law badge on him. They figured he'd make extraordinary efforts to deliver peace of sorts in a territory where lawlessness had held sway for too long.

Should he foul up in a situation like this,

the bad news would spread fast throughout the frontier lands. He'd be fair game for disrespect wherever he went. His unorthodox career could be ruined.

But he'd made his point successfully. After weighing his words and flanked by Axford's bouncers, the range riders took his advice and stumbled out of the saloon.

The less hot-headed, less inebriated of their number had convinced their comrades of the wisdom of a more-or-less orderly retreat. But they muttered profanities under their breath as they quit the scene of their aborted spree, fuming and frustrated. It was much harder to swallow pride than Axford's high-priced rotgut.

The hum and bustle of talk and drinking resumed in the Magnet. Behind the long bar, the five 'keeps were rushed off their feet supplying the liquor to slake throats parched by shouting and funk. The erstwhile merry-makers had hot new topics to discuss in the shape of the famous Lilly Honeydew's forced withdrawal and Joshua's shooting prowess.

Joshua was looking around with satisfaction at the restoration of normality, or a semblance of it, when he noted that sometime during the fracas, Billy McGee must have left his station at the bar.

He was nowhere in the hall. He'd vanished.

Joshua frowned. It wasn't like one of Blackie Dukes's boys to miss out on a mess of disorderliness. They'd rate it first-class entertainment, especially when it dragged in the despised ex-Pink and new town marshal.

It was while Joshua was conjecturing on this worrying riddle that it happened – a woman's piercing scream rose above the commotion, bringing it to a sudden halt. But the pause was momentary before general discourse picked up with a redoubled, speculative vigour.

Joshua placed the source of the scream somewhere back of the stage. And taking a guess, he put its origins in the same strong lungs that powered the soprano voice of

Lilly Honeydew.

The anguished scream was repeated.

What the hell was going on now?

# 10

## CUTTING DOWN THE ODDS

Joshua approached the stage at a run. Placing a hand on the platform, he vaulted athletically on to its boards. He stormed through the curtain-masked, open doorway at the rear. The red velvet swished behind him and he rushed on into the maze of gloomy passages behind.

The layout here was one Magnet feature that hadn't changed over the years. Joshua burst into the dance-girls' dressing-room, allotted exclusively to Miss Lilly Honeydew for the duration of her engagement.

A dramatic scene was presented to his

astonished gaze.

Two men, faces red-blotched from blows and anger, stood toe-to-toe exchanging hard-knuckled blows. One was Ramon Betzinez; the other Billy McGee. Even as Joshua arrived, a third dishevelled combatant, no less than the sweet-voiced Lilly Honeydew herself, tried to force herself between them for what was apparently not the first time.

'*No!*' she pleaded, her back to Joshua. 'You'll only get yourselves hurt.'

Betzinez swatted her aside with a vicious, backhanded cuff. She went sprawling. Her coiled blonde hair came unpinned and its tresses fell forward over her face like a golden waterfall. She screamed again but gamely scrambled to her feet, shaking her dazed head.

'Keep out of it, Miss Honeydew,' Joshua snapped. He joined the fight – and forced himself between the two men.

Billy McGee backed off, but said, '*You* keep outa it, lawman! This is private business.'

The trigger-tempered Betzinez was more assertive. 'Dead right. No two-bit, back-blocks marshal butts into my affairs!'

'You'd better learn how to show respect for authority,' Joshua said.

Betzinez snorted. 'Not when over-amorous buffoons can force their way into a celebrity's dressing-room, Marshal. Your law allowed this runt to act familiar and assault my wife!'

'How in blazes was I–?'

Joshua broke off. McGee's indignation was reignited – either by Betzinez's charge or the insulting appellatives. He surged forward again, this time brandishing his frightening bowie knife.

'Let's see the colour of your blue blood, 'breed,' McGee taunted.

Joshua leaped aside to dodge the flashing blade.

Betzinez went in the other direction, to snatch up his cane from where it lay on a table among the pots of powder and paint under a smeary mirror.

Joshua kept watching McGee, whom he considered the more dangerous of the hotheads, armed as he now was. But from a corner of his eye, he saw Betzinez twist his cane's silver knob and draw it away from the ebony body. Suddenly, there was a glitter of lamplight on cold steel.

Attached to the cane's decorative ferrule, Betzinez had a murderous-looking blade of his own, fully as long as McGee's bowie.

The showman's fingers curled round the silver hilt. Again, Joshua was forced to take a sidestep as he lunged at McGee.

Lilly uttered a cry of horror. All Joshua could glimpse of her face was a pallid mask of stage makeup behind her fallen hair.

McGee ducked under the sweep of Betzinez's dagger, stabbed upwards and ripped the sleeve of his opponent's coat.

Betzinez grunted in pain and retreated a step or two. Joshua saw blood on his exposed brown forearm – deep-red globules of it escaping in a jagged line from a shallow cut.

First strike to McGee, but a superficial

wound it seemed.

Betzinez attacked again. Blades clanged as the pair came together. Both were light on their feet; both had an unyielding and cruel nature.

Joshua wondered what had spurred the talented Lilly Honeydew to throw in with a man of Betzinez's ruthless calibre. Business considerations maybe, though it didn't seem enough. Just a mistake then?

Billy McGee was all killer from way back, despite his still youthful years.

More pressing demands took Joshua's all-encompassing attention. The duellists, so different in status yet equally matched in venom, were fencing to a decisive outcome with their short but menacing blades.

It was McGee's turn to gasp. Betzinez's wickedly sharp but rigid weapon ripped through McGee's shirt and sliced across his ribs. But McGee was nothing if not determined. He was incensed by the injury. 'Damn yuh, pimp! Yuh're gonna bleed for that. Yuh'll squeal fer mercy!'

They closed again. Joshua was hard put to see the opening to come between and separate them again. He wasn't prepared to sacrifice his life in a futile bid to stop the red-bladed violence.

He drew his revolver and reversed it in his fist, waiting for the right moment to deal one or other of their heads a clobbering blow with its solid butt that might end the conflict.

The chance never came.

Blades nicked into each other, locked, then grated as the sharp edges broke free. The sweating, cursing belligerents strived for the advantage at close quarters. With desperate fury, McGee raised his arm and slashed downward in a sweeping stroke intended to rip Betzinez open from throat to gut.

He was thwarted. To the accompaniment of sobs of dismay from Lilly, her husband blocked the swing of McGee's knife arm with his left, then plunged him into flaming agony with a short, powerful jab of his dagger-gripping right to the belly.

Betzinez's blade had to travel no further

than a foot to its target, but the affect was catastrophic from McGee's position. The fiery pain that followed the stabbing dagger's entry convulsed him and unclenched his grip on his knife, which clattered to the floor. He followed it instantly, thudding down in a foetal heap, clutching his gashed midriff.

'Drop your knife, Betzinez!' Joshua ordered.

But Betzinez didn't hear him, or ignored him. He crouched, bloody dagger ready, alert for a trick from McGee, unconvinced he'd dealt him a mortal blow. The wildness in his eyes made him look like a crazy man.

Joshua holstered his gun, clenched his teeth, stepped in and hit him. It was a devastating uppercut. Betzinez's back arched, he tottered back on his heels, arms spread wide and, with another floor-shaking thud, collapsed senseless.

Taking breath, Joshua blew on his punished knuckles and turned to McGee. He crouched beside him; saw the young thug was beyond help. 'Hell,' he said quietly.

Death didn't come much more gruesomely. Blood spewed through McGee's fingers as he pressed them against a spreading rupture through which it seemed his intestines threatened to spill.

Lilly had sat herself down at the dressing-table and plunged her face into her folded arms amidst the paraphernalia of her grooming. The mass of blonde hair formed a cover over most visible evidence of her emotions. But beneath the green gown her shoulders shook as she sobbed from shock or distress. Or maybe both. Joshua knew not what really, but she sounded like she was on the raw edge of hysteria. And it was certainly an upsetting experience for any young woman to witness.

'What was it all about, McGee?' Joshua asked. 'What did you do to Betzinez's wife, and why?'

McGee groaned. 'She ... she's not...'

'She's not what, man?' Joshua could tell the dying man had little time left to give his story.

Now the danger was passed, other folks were pushing into the dressing-room, demanding an explanation for Miss Honeydew's screams and the fight.

'What's going on in here?'

'Who attacked these men?'

'Shuddup!' Joshua snapped. McGee was struggling to speak.

'Ask ... her ... 'bout ... the ... the...'

It was too late. McGee's whisper gave out with a rattling sigh. His face froze. The light faded from his eyes. He was dead.

Joshua hadn't got any of the answers he wanted from McGee. But Ramon Betzinez and Lilly Honeydew would surely be able to fill in some of the details of what had been bugging the hardcase hell-raiser – if they chose.

Betzinez was helped to his feet by the Magnet bouncers. He looked like a man coming out of a deep sleep. His dark eyes were dazed, his jaw was swollen and blood dripped from his cut arm.

Joshua knew there was no way he'd be able

to question Betzinez the way he wanted here. The Latin artists'-agent was in no coherent state. Too many people were clustered around.

He considered whether there were grounds to arrest him and decided no. He and Cox City had enough woes without the hassles of litigation instigated by some smart metropolitan lawyer hired by the rich Betzinez. Personally, he had no money to pay damages; if they were successfully sued, the least inconvenience he could expect was a judge slapping garnishment on his wages.

'Take Mr Betzinez back to his hotel suite; Miss Honeydew likewise,' he told Axford's men. 'He ain't hurt that bad. Call a doc to patch him up if he wants. I'll visit with them later.'

He nudged McGee with a toe. 'And this one ... I guess he needs nobody but the undertaker.'

Joshua was anticipating trouble when he went to the Grand Western Montana Hotel.

He got it, though it was of a different sort from what he expected.

Ramon Betzinez and his talented wife had taken the best rooms in the brick-built establishment. The first intimation anything untoward was in train reached his ears as he ascended to the head of the carpeted stairs from the lobby.

It sounded unmistakably like the slap of an open hand on bare flesh, followed by a female cry.

Joshua hurried along the hotel corridor to the Betzinez's door, numbered 101, but lowered his knuckles at the last moment before they were about to rap on the varnished panel.

'You knew, you bitch!' he heard Betzinez say. 'You should never have gotten me to book you into this god-forsaken hole. Whatever did you have in mind? Tell me that, will you?'

A wail he interpreted as a negative was followed by another slap.

This was a serious spat. Whatever his

views on lawmen interfering in marital affairs, a man beating up on a woman was something he could not abide. Betzinez had given ample demonstration that he was a volatile man. Unstable, perhaps. Certainly he had an ugly, ruthless side that brooked no opposition to his will.

Joshua grasped the brass doorknob, turned it. Finding the door unlocked, he made an entry without announcement.

Lilly Honeydew lay on a bed. Her long blonde hair was in as much disarray as when he'd last seen her. It streamed over her face, at which she dabbed the big white square of a lace-fringed linen handkerchief. On seeing Joshua, she immediately buried her cheeks – one of which looked reddened, maybe by the marks of a slap – in its folds.

'Oh, God!' she cried. 'What more can go wrong?' Betzinez, reaching for her with a hand like a trembling claw, stopped and turned around.

He roared with rage. 'Get out! You can't come busting in here, sir!'

But Joshua hadn't come merely to take his leave. 'Mr Betzinez, I've questions I must ask you about the killing of William McGee at the Magnet. Howsoever, this further unpleasantness doesn't help your case.'

'My *case!*' Betzinez exploded. 'It was clear self-defence. And what goes on in the privacy of my hotel room has nothing to do with a busybody lawdog. So spare me your sermon, Dillard!'

He'd gone rigid with suppressed fury. His face was grey under its swarthiness and his dark eyes burned like he had a fever.

Joshua continued to remonstrate in even, firm tones. 'Miss Honeydew might be your wife, but in God's name you've no right to be using your man's hands to abuse her.'

'I'll do as I like,' Betzinez said, though managing to achieve a degree of self-control. 'Why, the woman owes everything to me. I picked her up off the streets, you know that? She had nothing. I've gotten her into the best opera houses and variety theatres in the nation. I've cut profitable deals, granted no concessions. I've *made* her. Now she repays me with secrecy and cheating and schemes of her own.'

Joshua edged further into the room, standing between Betzinez and the bed.

'What were you arguing about?' he asked Lilly, thinking she might be more disposed to explain matters to him.

She dabbed at her eyes with the voluminous handkerchief. 'It was my ... my selection,' she decided with a rush. 'Ramon insists I sing more Civil War and Stephen Foster songs, like "Swanee River".'

Betzinez was amused at the answer. A derisive noise escaped his loose lips.

Joshua knew she was covering up. He said, 'Be that as it may, I didn't come to discuss your performance.' To Betzinez, he added, 'I want to know why McGee came to Miss Honeydew's dressing-room and why it resulted in his death.'

Betzinez became sullen. 'I don't know. He raved some cock-and-bull story. I can tell you nothing. It made no sense and the slut won't explain.'

'I find your attitude unpardonable in a gentleman,' Joshua said. He put his back to the man. 'Miss Honeydew, I can help you if you'll help me.'

Betzinez blustered, 'That's a lie. You can do nothing for her, Dillard. Besides, she dare not go up against *me*. She'd be destitute inside of a season without my business expertise.'

Joshua avoided meeting the irate husband's smouldering gaze. 'Is this true?' he asked Lilly.

'Yes,' she mumbled into her handkerchief. 'A wife must be obedient. We can't help you. Go away, please.'

Joshua sighed heavily. 'This won't do you any good, ma'am. What'll become of you?'

'I'll be all right. There are – solutions. Just let me handle the situation my own way.'

# 11

## WHERE'S LILLY?

Joshua returned to his temporary office above the stone courthouse and accessed by an outside stairway. As he reached the half-built building, he came to a decision – the wrong one, it transpired.

Lilly Honeydew was in peril, and chiefly, it struck him, from her own scoundrel of a husband. Though handsome in a way, with skin-deep charm, he was vicious when crossed and smug when things went his way. Like McGee had suggested, he was little better than a pimp. He had no compunction about living on the earnings of a wife and client whose talents were receiving growing acclaim.

Joshua wanted an eye and an ear kept on

Betzinez and his battered wife. Being recognizable to them, and not free to abandon all other duties, he detailed a deputy, a man called Mahoney, to take up a discreet watch at the hotel.

'What do I look for, Marshal?' Mahoney asked.

Joshua didn't like to be too specific, knowing Lilly was reluctant to prefer charges. 'Oh, anything unusual. Disturbances arising. Just in case...'

'Yuh mean more Billy McGees? Admirers goin' off their heads?'

'Sure,' Joshua said. Protection from overzealous devotees to musical entertainment was as good a pretext as any for mounting a guard. 'Billy McGee was an admirer, was he?'

'Sort of, so it's said. Though no one's gotten to the bottom of it. People don't ask questions of Blackie Dukes an' his bunch, do they?'

'I expect now McGee's dead, a few who wouldn't breathe a word before will come right out and say good riddance to him.'

'That's fer sure. He was an ornery cuss with his mean pranks. Cocksure an' with a streak of cruelty. Prob'ly a killer, though we never proved anythin' ag'inst him. Reckon it was the kid who did for Pappy Jack back in the early Gulch days.'

'You could be right,' Joshua agreed. 'He finally got his needings anyhow.'

But somehow he found precious little satisfaction in the death. Dukes himself had yet to be accounted for, and instead of settling old mysteries, he'd had new ones dumped on his plate.

Nor had he yet unequivocally salvaged his tarnished reputation. In fact, it was possible events could be interpreted by the ungrateful as tending to bring it into further question. Had it been anyone other than McGee who'd gotten himself killed at the Magnet, he figured Mayor Miller and his council would already be on his tail, baying for his resignation.

Could Cox City be the unluckiest place in the whole West for him?

Joshua growled to himself. It was shaping up to be a difficult night. Maybe things would look better in the morning.

Joshua was disabused of his optimistic notion. Along with the early golden light of day came only fresh complications.

The first visitor to climb the stairway to his office, arriving before the stonemasons working on the new building, was Ramon Betzinez – in consternation and high dudgeon.

'What's become of her? Is this your doing?' he fumed.

'I haven't the least glimmering of what you're yammering about, Mr Betzinez. Why don't you take a seat and get your breath back?' Joshua indicated the leather armchair provided for visitors to the marshal's office.

Betzinez plumped himself into it, threw down his cane beside him and ran his hands through his unbrushed hair.

'My wife is missing. Unless you spirited her away for questioning, Dillard, I fear she's kidnapped in your lawless town!'

'Come, Mr Betzinez ... you're getting over-excited again. I had a man on guard in the hotel lobby all night. If there's been any abduction, I would've been told about it.'

Betzinez was not to be placated. He jumped back on his feet and rapped the top of the marshal's new desk with his cane. He did it so violently that he left a set of dimples in the polished woodwork.

'Then produce your man, Dillard! Let him tell us where Miss Honeydew is now.'

Unease churning in his as yet unbreakfasted stomach, Joshua accompanied the artists' agent to the Grand Western Montana.

The deputy was snoozing in a chair tucked away out of sight behind the desk clerk's counter.

'Mahoney! Mr Betzinez is reporting his wife missing,' Joshua said, coming straight to the purpose of his abrupt arrival.

The deputy came to his feet, blinking but instantly awake. 'Missing from where?'

'From our room here, you fool,' Betzinez said testily.

'Can't be,' Mahoney gave back. 'I've sat right in this spot all night and kept my eye on them stairs.'

'You were sleeping!' Betzinez accused.

'Nope,' Mahoney said. 'Just a sorta doze. Had my eyes half-open the whole time.'

Joshua took a deep breath and raised his eyebrows. 'Well, if she ain't upstairs, she must've come downstairs. And the hotel only runs to one flight of stairs.'

'Yuh're damn right, Mr Dillard. Them there. An' only one man's come down 'em since I bin set here. He didn't have no woman slung over his shoulder either.'

Betzinez was beside himself. 'This man is making fun of me, or he's an idiot. I'll see you lose your badge for this, Marshal! Miss Honeydew was in grave danger here. That was demonstrated by that ruffian McGee, but you failed to protect her.'

Joshua was astounded by the man's gall. If Lilly Honeydew had faced a threat to her safety, it was from the unconscionable cruelty of Betzinez's own behaviour.

He gave his attention to the deputy's report, such as it was. 'One man, Mahoney? What did he look like?'

The deputy scratched his head. 'Small to middlin' jasper, I guess. Very short dark hair, I remember that.'

'What did he wear? Range garb, city clothes?'

Mahoney's brows knit. 'Store clothes, I guess. A baggy coat an' pants. Like, real loose. Poor-fittin' stuff. Secondhand off a bigger feller mebbe.'

Joshua froze. The deputy's story had an eerily familiar ring to him. It tended to confirm a wild fancy that had already occurred to him, but which he'd discounted for its near-total improbability.

He paced the lobby. He had to clear his thoughts; put paid to any delusion triggered by his own past experience in this country.

Betzinez, increasingly disgruntled, said, 'Goddamnit, Marshal, can't you keep still? Better yet, why aren't you organizing a posse – or whatever it is you do in these primitive parts? Clearly, my wife's been snatched from under your deputy's nose by desperadoes!'

Mahoney, too, was starting to doubt himself. 'Say, Mr Dillard ... yuh reck'n this feller I saw was one of a kidnap gang in disguise?'

'No, I don't,' Joshua said. 'I reckon something quite different from that. Mr Betzinez, can we go up and have a look around your rooms?'

'You won't find her there, I told you that! You're wasting valuable time.'

'I hope you're wrong. Study on it, will you? Rushing all over the place like headless chickens would create another débâcle like the Magnet fracas. We need clues to point us in the right direction. They may be where Miss Honeydew was last known to be.'

Betzinez gave him a blank look. Joshua read contempt or disdain in his drooping lips before he grudgingly led them up to the empty suite.

The showman unlocked the door and threw it wide.

'Now then, Mr Smart-ass,' he said with a cynical laugh, 'how do you find a woman where you've been told she isn't?'

Joshua stepped into the first of the rooms, looked around, and peered through an open, connecting door to a second. He pointed to a closet fronted by carved doors.

'Are your clothes in there?' he asked.

'What if they are? A woman couldn't be hidden inside. I expect she'd suffocate.'

Joshua ignored his uncooperative attitude. He opened the closet.

'Why, you nosy–'

'Spare me your indignation, Mr Betzinez. Tell me, is one of your suits missing?'

Taken aback by the unexpectedness of the question, Betzinez was riffling through the hung clothing before he could frame a fresh objection.

He was miffed by what he found. 'By all the saints ... how did you know that?'

Joshua nodded in satisfaction. 'Remember? Someone left the hotel in ill-fitting garb. Maybe it was Miss Honeydew.'

Deputy Mahoney broke in. 'But it was a man, Marshal, with cropped, dark hair.'

'You were meant to think it was a man, Mahoney,' Joshua said, 'But let me ask Mr Betzinez one last question, which he mightn't appreciate.'

The doubt on Betzinez's swarthy features was transforming into renewed anger. He glared. 'I'll brook nothing impertinent, sir! I think what you're intimating is ridiculous.'

'My last question will settle that for any fair-minded observer equipped with a mite of logic.'

Betzinez shuffled uneasily and clenched his cane in both hands. 'Well, speak up. What is it, Dillard?'

But the anger still simmered inside him as he guessed at the enquiry Joshua was about to ask. 'However,' he rushed on, in a last attempt to save face, 'let me warn you that I will regard the divulgence of a professional and personal secret outside of these four walls as an infringement of my – and my wife and client's – rights. I will sue if Miss

Honeydew's character is destroyed.'

Joshua suppressed a surge of elation from showing as a smile. He knew what Betzinez's answer was going to be. Just as the showman had guessed the question.

'Mr Betzinez,' he said, 'is Miss Honeydew's magnificent blonde coiffure nothing more than a wig?'

# 12

## HOT SCENTS

Joshua was tempted by savoury smells wafting from a Main Street café. Ham, eggs and beans, washed down with strong black coffee, would go down a treat. His gut grumbled stridently when he passed the place by and pressed on to the largest and longest established of the Cox City livery barns.

If Lilly Honeydew had left town, that was

the place to start on her trail.

Checking out this craziness gave him an ominous sense of déjà vu. The feeling was heightened when he discovered the hostler on duty was Curtis Reisman, as hulking and vacant-eyed as he'd been seven years back. Why, Joshua could swear the fellow still wore the same old sheepskin coat over a rag-bag shirt and Levis just as unfamiliar with the washtub as their predecessors.

'Busy night, Reisman?'

'Naw. Real quiet. Sittin' at the desk ain't no fun in the small hours. Coulda had some pleasure with an easy woman up in the hayloft, had I known. I got me an offer, yuh know.'

Joshua doubted it, but said, 'Is that so? No other business at all?'

'Aw, now yuh mention it, Marshal, thar was a feller. Rented a trim black mare an' asked for directions to Eriksen's spread.'

'Wasn't it kinda late to go riding and visiting?'

'Waal, the moon was up an' I ain't paid to

ask questions. He had deposit money an' seemed in a helluva hurry.'

Joshua mentally cursed the dirty livery-man's indifference. Except for his boasted exploits with soiled doves, he lived in a stupor where nothing seemed to register.

'Who's this Eriksen, Reisman?'

'Rancher Eriksen. Small place off the stage road to Bannack. You know. He married that ol' upstairs girl who worked outa Axford's Magnet. Hannah Powell.'

'No, I didn't know. I was away from Cox City seven years in case you didn't notice. Anything else a lawman might want to hear about?'

Joshua's sarcasm was lost on Reisman. He yawned, raised his left arm and scratched under his armpit with the bitten fingernails of his stubby right-hand. Joshua didn't think he imagined the waft of foul body odour.

'Come to think of it, yeah... Moment this young feller hot-footed it on the black, another rider took out from the hitch rack front of the hotel. Blackie Dukes it was, I reck'n. I seen him sorta lurkin' thar when I came on shift.'

This and the tidbit about Eriksen and Hannah Powell were the only pieces of information Joshua could drag out of Reisman that did more than confirm his own guess-work. The additions to his knowledge not only deepened his convictions: they added fresh concerns.

'Kate Thompson! Unbelievable, but it has to be. With Blackie Dukes hot on her trail.'

Kate Thompson was taking another gamble. Like all the chances littered down the back-trail of her life, it loomed at this early stage like the largest ever. It was do or die, and now was the hour.

The years with Ramon Betzinez had promised so much at the outset. With his suave charm, he'd ably assisted her to forge a new identity and to make real money from her singing talents, to escape the round of boom-town residencies that had been pulling her to her ruin. But the promise had not lasted. She'd become, in effect, a captive to him, a slave to his will and his Latin tantrums. Being the great Lilly Honeydew was a little taste of hell. Marriage – a convenience he'd insisted upon – had only tightened the other bonds with which he'd trammelled her.

It was past time for Kate to throw off the shackles and reclaim her own life.

Her fate depended on what she found at the end of her moonlight ride down the stage road a fair piece toward Bannack. Already, much had gone horribly wrong since her recognition by Billy McGee. That, his death at Ramon's hand and the subsequent confrontation, had precipitated this hasty move.

The timing was awfully bad. Dogs barked as she approached the darkened ranch house.

Silvery light gave the property a starkness. But the spectral illumination aside, it looked run-down. Pole corral fences leaned drunkenly. An outbuilding – maybe a barn – was near collapse. The porch and the roofline of the house sagged in the middle. Clumps of porcupine grass sprouted as weeds in the yard.

The Eriksens were no better than poor dirt-farmers. Yet how could this be? What had become of the fortune Kate had left in Hannah's safekeeping? Surely her old friend hadn't squandered it all, or lost it? Had it been taken off her? Every one of her rapid thoughts seemed an unlikely explanation, unless Hannah had greatly changed.

Hannah was a fighter and intensely loyal. As custodian of the gold taken from Axford's safe, she would have relinquished it only at her death.

In the house, a man yelled to the dogs and a kerosene lamp was evidently lit. The crooked square of a window glowed a yellowish orange. Kate reined in on the edge of the yard and waited in plain view in the moonlight. She had no need to hullo the house. The dogs had announced her arrival for her.

They came bounding up, three Alsatian-crosses, snarling fiercely, denying her entry to the house's precincts. The black shied and snorted, but Kate tightened the reins and controlled her with a soothing word.

The door of the house opened, spilling more light, and a man appeared, clad in a night-shirt and clutching a shotgun.

'Goddamnit! Who the hell are you out there at this wretched hour? What do you want? This is a scatter-gun I've got here, plumb loaded with big buckshot. I'd rather you rode on without my having to use it.'

Kate swallowed as she sat her head-shaking, tail-frisking horse. 'My name is Kate Thompson and I'm an old friend of Hannah Powell. Are you Mr Eriksen?'

The dogs recommenced their barking at the sound of her strange voice.

'A woman...' the man said wonderingly, perplexed by her male attire and riding seat. He took some steps toward his tumbledown barn and bellowed, 'All right, you critters, that's enough! Come here!'

The dogs quietened their baying belligerence to a whimper or two. Then their owner led them to the barn and dragged open the door. They followed at an eager trot, sniffing. The man took up a cleaver and hacked a hunk of meat off a carcass hung from a high hook just inside and threw it down. The dogs fell to a tussle over its disposal; the man addressed himself to the untimely visitor's enquiry.

'Yeah, I'm Eriksen an' Hannah's my wife. Mebbe you'd better step down an' come on in. I figure some explainin' is due.'

'Oh, a great deal, Mr Eriksen, if it pleases you.'

Whether it pleased him or not, it pleased Hannah, who met them at the door.

'Kate ... Kate Thompson, by all that's holy! I can't believe it. I thought I might never see you again.'

After she'd gotten over the shock, she was delighted to be reunited with her old Magnet partner.

In a homely parlour, Kate was properly introduced to Lars Eriksen. He was a big-bellied, red-faced but abstemious ex-miner who'd never struck it rich but had had the nous to get out while the getting was good. He'd invested his pile of dust in improving a few hundred acres of dirt that yielded him a regular income, supplying assorted produce to a growing town market.

He'd also seen the worth in taking Hannah Powell as his bride – a tough, strongly built woman willing to help work his land and eager to put a sinful life behind her. In fact, Hannah confessed, she was amazed to be given the chance and had conquered the Demon Drink to take it.

Eriksen had his confession, too: after a couple of nights' educative lovemaking with his new wife, he would have 'crawled across a mountain in blizzard' to get to her.

Kate, who had her own memories of mountain blizzards, told of her less happy circumstances, making little of her fame as Lilly Honeydew, but emphasizing her determination to leave it all behind and flee the clutches of her violent husband and the rigours of a palling career in vaudeville.

Outside, shut in the barn, the three dogs went to barking once more. Eriksen went to the house door and hollered for silence again. 'Pesky dogs,' he muttered. 'Sorry 'bout that.'

Kate picked up her story. 'I tricked Ramon into bringing me to Cox City, despite his complaints that it was an out-of-way place not worthy of his artiste. I needed to get here to see you. And, of course, to collect the wherewithal to bankroll my life's second great escape.'

'But Kate,' Hannah said, a look of distress coming to her now much-lined but somehow less hard face, 'I don't know if you can, whether it would be right.'

'What do you mean? What became of our gold?'

Hannah's chin quivered, as in the old days. 'Well, first of all, I hid it in the sludge at the bottom of my old cabin's rain barrel. Right off, it was almost found when Blackie Dukes and his scum came calling and cruelly attacked me, but I was saved at the last moment by Joshua Dillard, the Pinkerton man.'

Kate felt twinges of guilt, thinking of how she'd fooled the lawman at that time and again this very day. Or was it yesterday?

She said, 'By unfortunate timing, Mr Dillard has turned up in Cox City again – as the new town marshal, arriving just shortly before me, I do believe.'

'Sure,' said Eriksen. 'We heard 'bout that. A grim jasper nowadays, they do say. Bad men plenty places else have ganged up on him, ambushed him, beat the living daylights outa him, reckoned him fixed fer certain sure. But he bobs up ag'in, tracks 'em down an' dishes out the punishment, to hell with legal process. A man o' conscience, I figure, but tough an' smart...'

'Oh, a very resolute and perceptive man who has good reason to remember me, Mr Eriksen,' Kate said. 'However, by various subterfuges I've endeavoured to hide my face from him at every juncture, and now I've given him the slip again. But I interrupted, Hannah ... the gold?'

'I daren't try to cash up any of it after I fell under suspicion, or only very little. Dukes and his boys watched me like hawks for ages, I'm sure. Later, when I married, I brought it here. And Lars convinced me we shouldn't touch even my share, though God knows we could've used it.'

This sounded to Kate like Hannah taking her reformation, and Eriksen his principles, a mite too far. 'Why on earth not?'

'Because it wasn't what we thought. It wasn't Aces Axford's ill-gotten gains from the exploitation of us girls at all: it was the pokes of hard-working miners deposited with the skunk for keeping in his safe in the days before Cox City had a bank!'

Kate was flummoxed at the knowledge. It had been denied her so long ... and all the while she'd weaved her dreams.

'How do you know this?' she asked.

Hannah answered with another question. 'Didn't the one pouch you took have a slip of paper stuffed into its neck?'

'Why, yes, it did, but I couldn't understand why Axford had it in his safe. It was a quotation from the Bible – Leviticus – and Aces never acted as though he had any deep religious convictions.'

Eriksen asked, 'Can you remember the passage, ma'am?'

'It said. "And all the tithe of the land, whether of the seed of the land, or of the fruit of the tree, is the Lord's: it is holy unto the Lord." And it gave chapter and verse, which I've forgotten off-hand.'

Eriksen nodded his ponderous head slowly. 'A claim-worker of a devout turn of mind must have put it there anonymously. It was probably a tenth of his dust and he intended it to be passed on to a church someplace as payment of tithes. The slips in all the other pouches bore Gulch miners' names.'

'Oh, no!' Kate gasped. 'Well – that is, I mean yes. I'm beginning to see.'

Hannah shrugged, as though even now she was helpless. 'I felt that my hands were tied until I could talk to you again.'

Eriksen said in a low, growly voice, 'I'm

dead ag'inst you gals divvyin' the gold up. The whole kit-an'-caboodle should've been handed back somehow.'

'Yes, of course, maybe it should...'

'But I can't figure no safe way to do it without implicatin' Hannah an' you. A body da'sn't. The lawmen in this country have always tended to be blasted crooks theirselves. I couldn't bear to have my wife taken away and locked up in a penitentiary to rot, while scoundrels creamed off a take from the pickin's.'

Kate had gambled on the strength of a card she thought she had tucked up her sleeve. Her bid to secure her future looked doomed to fail.

Blackie Dukes, tall and lean, crept on to the Eriksens' porch and cat-footed to a spot beneath the parlour window. Without an ounce of spare flesh anywhere on his rail-like frame, he could move across the dried-out, cracked boards with scarcely a sound.

He chuckled to himself evilly. Right convenient how obedient Eriksen's hounds were to their owner. He'd shut 'em up good with his last hollering for silence.

The warped window frame meant the sash was permanently ajar. Brushing his lank black hair away from his ear, Dukes put his gaunt skull up to the crack and heard everything said in the Eriksens' parlour. What the one-time wolf of the goldfields learned filled him with chagrin and anger. The whore Powell had had the gold from the Magnet all along!

And Billy McGee – stupid big kid though he'd been – had gotten it right about Lilly Honeydew. She was the Kate Thompson he'd sparked and who'd double-crossed them back in the old days.

The kid had said he'd known those tits the moment he'd bared them when they'd held up the stage from Bannack. No wonder really – he'd spent enough hours in the past drinking Axford's rotgut and staring down Kate's shapely bosom!

These hicks the Eriksens had had him

fooled for a considerable spell, working their poverty-stricken holding while hanging on to the unspent loot from the Magnet that was rightly his and the gang's. But no never-mind about that now. It was payback and pay-up time, just as soon as he could get the bunch together and ride out here again in full force to claim it.

They'd show 'em the what-for of things. Poor Billy would have enjoyed making the Thompson bitch scream, too. Pity he'd gone off half-cocked. Still, he'd enjoy taking the chore on board his ownself. After seven years, the ex-saloon girl was young flesh yet: still looked a purty tasty dish. In fact, he suspicioned she had a mite more meat on her bones, a condition he'd check out, personal.

There'd be fun as well as gold. 'Miss Honeydew' was surely gonna sing one more time...

# 13

## THE GANG ATTACKS

In morning's light the leather and canvas pouches of gold were heaped on the Eriksens' deal table.

'None of it's worth a damn to us,' Eriksen grumbled. 'I don't cotton to payin' my bills with other folks' fortunes. It's a *liability*.'

It was as Kate had been told – each pouch had a slip of paper tucked into a usually draw-stringed top. The slips were crumpled, dirty, water-stained and mostly illegible, but clearly they were names and none of them was 'Axford'.

'If not in his safe, where did the crafty ol' bastard keep his own loot?' Hannah complained.

'Ain't no use to bellyache 'bout it, my love.'

Eriksen said. 'You gals took a mighty big risk. You was lucky to git off with your lives. Blackie Dukes was a murderer, an' still is, I opine. Thank God he's never gotten on to us. It was good that Dillard chased him off with his gun that night at Hannah's cabin.'

Hannah grinned. 'I think Blackie was convinced I knew nothin' after he'd upended me in the rain barrel and I still failed to talk. To think, the torturin' swines were so near to their gold, yet so far!'

'As close a call as any I've had,' Kate said.

The rueful reminiscing went no further.

Noise outside, including the barking of the three dogs shut up in the barn, indicated that riders were surrounding the ranch house.

Kate's heart started to beat faster with a sudden foreboding that her schemes were coming unstuck with a vengeance.

Eriksen said, 'Now what? Whoever can this be? Put that pesky stuff out of sight, Hannah.'

From the yard, a harsh voice hollered. 'Eriksen! Are you there?'

'Blackie Dukes!' Hannah cried, her eyes wide with surprise and horror. 'Why has he come here...? An' now of all the times!'

'Step on out, Eriksen!' Dukes called.

'Not a word,' Eriksen hissed to the women. 'Don't even move.'

'We know you're up an' around in there,' Dukes said, his voice getting uglier, rougher. 'Smoke's a-curling outa your tin chimney.'

Kate glanced at the stove, freshly banked up and with a coffeepot sizzling on the plate.

Dukes waited. When he was given no response, he sounded even more impatient.

'Last chance, Eriksen. Open that door and no one gets hurt. Leastways, not *bad*.'

Sniggers from those with him made mockery of his promise.

'We ain't bluffing, mister!' Dukes shouted. 'This is the business. Get your ass out here, an' bring them two whores with you!'

Eriksen grabbed up his shotgun and cocked back the hammers. 'No bastard calls my wife a whore,' he growled.

'Lars!' Hannah said jerkily. 'For God's

sake, be careful!' But her warning went un-heeded. Eriksen hauled open the ranch house door and moved out on to the porch, his bulky figure all aggression.

The instant Dukes saw the shotgun, he knew he'd underestimated his man. He shrilled, 'Kill him!'

Dukes and the three surviving members of his gang who accompanied him fired simul-taneously from where they sat their horses lined up in front of the dilapidated house.

Eriksen was knocked off his feet and hurled back into the doorframe by the impact of the four bullets. But not before he let loose with the shotgun.

Two of Dukes's men and a horse were cut down in a sudden, misty shower of blood and a frenzied tumult of human and equine squealing.

'The sonofabitch!' Dukes howled in in-credulous fury. 'He's mowed down Brad an' Fats.'

Eriksen's dropped shotgun crashed on to the sprung porch planks. The rancher himself slid down the door frame, his legs folding and his out-of-control arms flapping. He crumpled into a still, grotesque heap, his limbs at unnatural angles. Trickles of deep-red blood coursed from the entry and exit holes in his body across the weather-greyed timber.

The girls began screaming and over in the barn the dogs kicked up a fearsome racket, flinging their heavy bodies against its rickety door and mouldering walls.

The cold-blooded Dukes spared no time on attending to Brad and Fats. They'd been reduced to doll-rags by the awesome swathe through man and horse cut by the ten-gauge's twin loads.

'C'mon, Lou,' he snapped. 'Let's get at them gals an' the gold!'

When Joshua Dillard heard gunfire in the direction where he thought the isolated Eriksen property might he situated, he put his horse off the regular trail and to a gallop across the dew-soaked bluestem grassland.

The sun was climbing the eastern sky; grooved tracks through the wet grass showed plainly in its slanting light. He was reassured that he was following the right path and worried by the tracks' significance. Others had passed this way lately on swift hoofs. Four riders, he judged.

He had a shrewd reckoning that his presence was required urgently, and he hoped the course he was cutting was the best one and would save him valuable minutes. They might mean the difference between life and death. Also the success or otherwise of his unusual posting as a peace officer in Montana, and then, in turn, the resolution of issues that had bothered him seven long years.

Like Blackie Dukes before him, he saw the smoke from the Eriksens' chimney first. It wasn't the thin, spreading strata of a fire banked up for overnight, but the rising billows of a household up and breakfasting. That gave him the bearing he sought, and he kneed his mount on faster.

Cresting a ridge and bursting into a shallow valley, he saw the place ahead of him. Three horses stood on dropped reins while a third was lying in the dust and – for Christ's sake – giving feeble twitches with dying legs and straining to lift its neck. The red-streaked corpses of two men were quite inert.

Joshua resisted the temptation to thunder down the slope. He approached cautiously. The self-generated, rushing din of his passage ceased. He heard the barking of the frantic dogs. He heard the anguished cries of women...

In the yard, he dismounted silently and drew his Peacemaker. He ran to the house, where another man's body was heaped at the door like a burst sack of corn. He relied on the barking and the hubbub of what was happening in there to mask his approach.

Snatches of excited phrases and struggle reached his ears: 'How about we both mount her?' A gasp of female horror. 'What?' A rip of clothing. An appreciative laugh. A stifled moan.

Joshua delayed no longer. He went in. It looked like he'd be one man against two, but surprise was on his side.

Hannah Powell was curled up on the floor, partially unclothed, her face bruised, and near comatose in a state of deep shock and distress.

Kate Thompson had been put down on all fours between two men: a grunting Blackie Dukes and the thug Joshua knew as Lou. She was still fighting back, but they had her trapped and held, partly in the tangles of her own disarranged clothing.

'Yee-haw! This is gonna be good,' Lou said.

'No, it ain't,' Joshua rapped. He gave him no chance to defend himself. He shot him without ceremony in the upper thigh.

Lou dropped his hold on Kate and yelled like a Comanche.

But Blackie Dukes was smart and quick as a striking snake. He tugged to him the woman they'd been assaulting, pulling her up by the constricting remnants of a man's baggy suit.

Joshua dared not shoot again as Dukes made Kate Thompson his shield and hefted his six-gun from his belt in a bony fist.

'Easy, Dillard. Drop your gun, or Mrs High Notes will be singing with the angels.'

Joshua cursed but did as Dukes demanded.

'Now kick it over to me!' the thin lips spat. 'Remember, the upper hand is mine here. I've got nothing to lose.'

Again, Joshua complied as Dukes jerked Kate still closer to him.

Dukes stooped, swept up the new-model Peacemaker and stuck it in his belt. Shuffling backwards, and never taking his eyes off Joshua for a moment, he reached the table and picked up a sack there that had been stuffed full with pouches.

'You'll never get away from here alive, I swear,' Joshua said. 'Let alone with a bag of gold and a woman hostage.'

'We'll see about that,' Dukes grated. With the neck of the sack and his revolver in one hand, and his other arm tight around Kate's neck, he backed out on to the porch.

Joshua had his moves figured. The weak point in Dukes's evident plan of escape was going to be when he went to put his captive on horse and mount up. He'd take his chance then to rush the sidewinder.

But Joshua's intentions were undone by a damnable piece of ill-luck. Dukes had gotten past the barn, and Joshua was edging after him, apparently unarmed and helpless, when it happened and his stratagem was reduced to ruins.

Eriksen's fretting hounds, stirred to fresh agitation by the movements nearby, finally burst through the barn door, smashing it down along with a section of the rotting wall. They immediately saw Joshua and cornered him, yapping and snarling.

Meanwhile, Dukes was free to throw a stunned Kate over his saddle-bow. He laughed at Joshua's predicament.

Weaponless, Joshua could only yell at the angry dogs and retreat from their fangs. Then he saw the carcass hanging inside the now very open barn, and the cleaver on the chop-scarred workbench below.

It was time for bold, decisive action of the type at which Joshua was adept.

Chased by the dogs, Joshua ran into the barn. In a trice, he took up the cleaver and sliced a juicy portion off the carcass. He flung it into the animals' midst. The clever tactic worked. The dogs' attentions were diverted; they'd gotten easier meat to rend and tear.

Still holding the bloody cleaver, Joshua rushed back into the yard. Dukes was in the saddle and clapping his heels to a refractory horse.

Joshua threw the cleaver. It went end over end, ten inches of hard steel glinting as it caught the sunlight, hurtling through the air.

It thudded into Dukes's back, chopping him from the saddle. He landed front down in the dust, striving ineffectively to reach behind him and feel what it was that had struck him.

A look of bafflement and hatred contorted his bony features.

# 14

## ACES IN A HOLE

The cleaver had struck Blackie Dukes dead-centre between the shoulder blades. It had embedded itself, deeply and vertically, the sharp cutting edge first. Only the wooden haft and a narrow band of the metal was visible, projecting from his back. Surprisingly little blood was seeping from the wound past the makeshift weapon's obstruction.

Joshua crouched beside him, supporting him. 'You're done for, Dukes. You'll be dead in minutes, I reckon. No one can survive four by ten inches of cold steel driven into his back. Is there anything you want to say?'

Dukes fixed his executioner with stony gaze. 'Yeah. It's this – you ain't the feller who won, Mr Clever Pinkerton Dick.'

'I'm not a Pinkerton any more, Dukes.'

'Marshal then,' the hell-raisers' leader jeered, sweat beading his brow. 'Same difference. Just a dammed fool at the start an' at the finish.'

'About winning – what do you mean?'

Time was running out for Dukes. Unless he spoke now, Joshua might never know.

'Aces won. Mebbe the gals, if they got the guts to take the gold offa you. But Aces mostly. He's up there still. Cox City's big man; the mastermind, foxing you entire...'

A gurgling sound put paid to any more of his diatribe. A froth of pink bubbled from his mouth. The silence and stillness of death claimed him.

Frowning, feeling cheated of something important, Joshua lowered Dukes to the ground and pulled his hat over his frozen white face, more skull-like than ever.

Kate was struggling to get down from the restive horse and he went to help her.

'No, I'm all right, thank you,' she said, finally coping and slipping to the ground.

'But they killed Mr Eriksen and what they did to Hannah ... I must go help her.'

Limping slightly, she headed to the house. Joshua followed.

Inside the house, the hard case Lou was groaning and trying to make a tourniquet for his punctured upper leg with his belt. 'Go fetch me a doc!' he blurted, his face twisting up with pain.

Kate ignored him and went to comfort Hannah. Eriksen's widow was sitting on the floor, sobbing pitifully.

Joshua said to Lou, 'You don't need a sawbones. The slug passed right through.'

'Hell! I do, Dillard. I'm bleedin' to death. The bone's busted. I'll be a cripple. You gotta help me.'

Joshua regarded him poker-faced. 'In time, maybe we will. If we think a louse like you is worth saving.'

Fear joined the pain in Lou's wet eyes. 'I need a medic,' he sobbed.

'And I need information,' Joshua said implacably. 'How about we do a trade?'

'Sure, sure,' Lou said, shaking and pale. 'What d'you wanna know?'

'Blackie Dukes is dead. He was telling me Aces Axford was a "mastermind" and I was fooled, but he didn't finish. What did he mean?'

'Aces bankrolled us – the gang,' Lou said. 'He ran all the rackets as well as the Magnet. He was behind the robberies an' hold-ups an' muggin's. In the old days, he was no sympathizer of the Republican Governor Sidney Edgerton at all. That was just a blind. Likewise, you as a Pink an' sent by Edgerton was used as window-dressing. Aces had links with the crooked Henry Plummer, who was a Democrat.'

Joshua dredged up from his memory what he knew of the notorious Plummer, politician, one-time Sheriff of Bannack and secret bandit chief. The crook had been hanged in 1864 by vigilantes. If Axford was cast from the same devious mould, it would explain a lot.

'Go on,' Joshua said. 'You'll have to tell me

more than that.'

Lou gulped. 'Blackie an' us was workin' for Axford when we plotted to take the gold from his safe. It weren't his gold, yuh see. Not a damn' scrap – jest miners' savings banked with him – but he was goin' to make it his, or a big cut of it. An' he shot deputy Steve Wye deliberate, 'cos he was gettin' too smart an' demandin' – makin' a nuisance of hisself.'

Joshua feigned scepticism. 'How do I know this is anything but a crock of moonshine?' he said, shrugging.

'It's what Blackie said,' Lou maintained, going grey and sweaty. 'I can prove Aces don't keep his own loot in his safe. He keeps it in a locked steel ammo box under his office floorboards. Does to this day, an' always has. No one knows that 'cept his closest cronies – fellers like Blackie.'

Joshua figured he'd learned as much as Lou could tell – and enough to bring the whole staggering, drawn-out business to a successful conclusion.

'All right,' he said. 'We'll get you to town and a doctor. We'll get your statement written up and you can sign it in exchange for medical expenses.'

A buckboard was wheeled out from the back of Eriksen's barn. Lou, Hannah and the sack of gold were loaded on to the freight tray. Joshua and Kate climbed up to the seat, he shook the lines and they jogged off, heading for town.

'I feel so sorry for Hannah,' Kate said, then suggested tentatively. 'Perhaps we should let her have some of the gold, Marshal.'

'And how would she explain she'd come by that?' Joshua asked.

Kate pondered. After a moment, she said brightly, 'She could say a rich uncle had left her the gold in his will.'

Hannah had been listening while quietly nursing her grief. She scoffed. 'No one would believe it. Only rich "uncle" I ever had was one of them kinds as has three balls over the front sign of his store.'

'Nope. It won't do, ma'am,' Joshua said. 'I have a duty. That gold must go back to its rightful owners if they can be traced. As for Aces Axford, he must be exposed and brought to fair trial.'

'Of course,' Kate said, and lapsed into a shamefaced silence which endured until they reached the outskirts of Cox City, where she raised a new objection.

'I can't possibly return to the hotel, Mr Dillard. Ramon will be furious. He'll probably beat me.'

'Hmmm ... that is a problem. I'd forgotten about your abusive husband.'

'Well, I haven't. It was the reason I came to Cox City. To claim the gold I knew Hannah would be keeping for me, and to use it to escape from his clutches.'

Joshua shook his head wonderingly. 'It was a wild scheme. No wonder it didn't work out. Didn't you think you might be recognized?'

'I did think there was a chance, but I could think of no other way to get the money to finance my flight and freedom. Besides, it wasn't such a huge risk to take. I'm older now and must have changed a lot.'

Joshua laughed. 'Hardly! It was the wig and the stage-type face paint that made the biggest difference.'

Kate would not be convinced. 'But the Magnet must have had thousands of saloon girls pass through its doors in seven years. They come and they go. Don't I know it?'

She paused as a new line of defence occurred to her. 'Besides, who would have imagined that Billy McGee would have held up the very coach I came in and seen me at close quarters? Or that a certain ex-Pinkerton detective would be taken on as the new town marshal?'

'Yeah, I have to grant you that, though the Dukes bunch held up coaches aplenty and regular. The rest wasn't anything a body could predict either.'

'What I can predict is that Ramon Betzinez is going to be a beast to me. Can't you help me?'

'Sorry, ma'am,' Joshua said. 'I ain't got any

place to keep a runaway wife. 'Less you want me to put you in one of the city's cells!'

Kate's face lit up. 'Why, that's a perfectly splendid idea! I'd be safe there, wouldn't I?'

'It'd do as a temporary solution, I guess ... while we worked out something more permanent. But how would I explain it?'

'You could tell the truth, more or less – say I'd been involved in the killings at Eriksen's ranch; that I was being held for further questioning by someone coming from the county sheriff's office.'

'Or that seven years ago you stole thirty-five thousand dollars of gold off the Gulch miners.'

'I didn't know!' Kate protested. 'I thought it was stuff Axford had earned by using girls and cheating folks. That he didn't deserve to have it. And now we've testimony that he was behind the thieves I double-crossed. A murderer, too.'

Joshua stopped teasing her ... though he still felt a mite peevish about how she'd fooled him back then, skipping out and leaving him stranded in a blizzard in the Bitterroots.

'All right. You can be my guest in jail. Betzinez will have a hard job getting at you there.' He patted her hand reassuringly and she gave him a thankful smile in return.

In Cox City, Joshua left Hannah Powell with a woman friend she named, who also kindly supplied Kate with some women's clothes. Betzinez's suit, somewhat the worse for wear, was tied in a bundle for Joshua to return to him later.

But that was low on his list of priorities.

Kate and Lou were left with Deputy Mahoney at the marshal's office and jail, one storey up at the new courthouse. A doctor was called to dress Lou's bullet wound and a lawyer to write down his statement. Joshua explained to Mahoney that Kate was not an actual prisoner, but staying in the cells for protection from her violent husband.

Joshua then returned the rented black mare to Curtis Reisman at the livery barn. 'So yuh caught up with the feller?' the hostler said.

Joshua didn't waste any time satisfying the dirty oaf's idle curiosity. With the chores done, he was anxious to get down to the real business – to confront and arrest Aces Axford on charges of robbery and murder.

Axford's ascending fortunes had allowed him to build a fine, nine-room frame residence on a cross street a stone's throw from the Magnet. It had tall, shuttered windows and wide porches both front and back. Small, sunny balconies jutted out from the upper floor.

A black manservant answered Joshua's knock. 'Why, Mistah Dillard, yo' sure is early. I guess the mastah won't hardly be woken yet. He done work late hours at the salo'n, as yo' know.'

'The business is urgent, my friend,' Joshua said.

'Suppose yo' come inside an' wait a spell.'

The servant tripped off, muttering to himself 'Mistah Axford sure gonna be powerful grumpy … must be mighty impo'tant can't wait for gentlemen t' eat breakfas'.'

Joshua called after him, 'Tell him the Blackie Dukes gang is busted up and the marshal is getting a full, signed statement on its doings from Lou Halloran.'

He was shown upstairs into the master's presence almost instantly. Axford was dressed for the street and his saloon. It seemed the protective – or well-trained – servant had been exaggerating a mite about late breakfast-taking.

Without preliminaries, Joshua said briskly, 'I'd like to talk to you in private, Axford.'

'Sure, Marshal, I'd like to talk some myself. Mayor Miller ain't at all happy about the riot at the Magnet. That'll be all, Thomas.'

When Thomas had departed, the saloon man waved his visitor to a chair. 'Set down, Joshua. Smoke?'

Axford had to be rattled. His cryptic but telling message had been delivered. Of that, Joshua was sure from his quick admission, but he was playing it cool to the last.

'I think not, Axford. This isn't a social call

and we won't be here long.'

Axford struck a match and put it to a cheroot. A ghost of a smile played on the lips under the curved, waxed moustache. 'You don't say? Then where will we be?'

'We'll be over to the jailhouse and you'll be in a cell, awaiting trial for murder, conspiracy and robbery.'

Axford blew his stinking smoke at Joshua. 'Because of some bullshit story from a known hell-raiser, I take it. Oh, you can hear all kinds of tales in this town. Some folks – losers like yourself – are so down on a successful businessman. And they're scared witless of Dukes, whose gang has bust up, you say.'

'Been shot up,' Joshua said grimly. 'Dukes himself is dead, too, but he confessed first, and I have a member of his gang who'll be a prosecution witness. You'll be shown as a liar, a thief and a murderer, of a type I purely hate to see. Your game's up, Axford.'

The saloon man snorted irritably 'And you're a hired gun passing himself off as a lawman. D'you really think such dubious evidence will get a conviction against a man who's a pillar of the community?'

'It'll get you up the gallows steps, Axford. I'm taking you in for the murder of Deputy Steve Wye, for conspiring to appropriate miners' gold, and for complicity in other deaths and crimes.'

Joshua assumed it was shock at the extent and detail of his knowledge that put Axford to coughing on the smoke of his foul cheroot. Choking, Axford dropped the ashy butt and reached for the white handkerchief tucked showily into the top pocket of his coat.

But it proved a pretence – a feint that allowed Axford to draw a sneak gun hidden behind the loose silk folds in the same top pocket.

It was a slightly dated, four-shot Remington derringer with a blued-steel finish made to the William Elliot patents of 1860 and 1861.

Axford drew and fired. But he'd acted too fast and, like for many an inexpert gunfighter, his haste proved to be at the expense of accuracy.

His shot tore through Joshua's left coat-sleeve, inflicting a painful graze that burned like blazes, but was nothing more than a skin-deep injury.

Joshua's reflexes were lightning-fast. Even as Axford's derringer showed, he was hauling out his big new Peacemaker.

Axford panicked. He had three shots left, but instead of triggering again, his instinct was to take flight from a man he feared was a superior marksman and who had what looked a bigger, better gun.

He reached the tall window in a single bound. It was unlatched and opened on to one of the house's small balconies. The delicate material of the fluttering drapes caught at him like spiders' webs and ripped as he rushed through.

Joshua fired his Peacemaker, but Axford was too fast for him, and gone. He was rewarded with only the smash of broken glass. By the time he'd reached the balcony himself, Axford had jumped or swung himself down and was lurching across the street on what Joshua supposed was a sprained ankle to a hitch rack.

Axford turned to fire a second shot from his derringer – and a second miss – before he jerked loose the reins of a standing buckskin, put his foot into the left stirrup, jumped on to the horse and sent it bolting up the street.

'Damnation!' Joshua cursed. 'He's gonna get away!'

He aimed and triggered again. It was a longish shot for a handgun, but his hopes were buoyed when Axford involuntarily stiffened.

The chancy shot had hit him in the back at waist level.

Aces Axford wasn't finished yet. Not by a long chalk, he vowed to himself. He groaned and gritted his teeth. The pain that had knifed into his vitals as the heavy slug had struck him was almost crippling. But he kept kicking his heels into the buckskin's flanks and they stormed on pell-mell out of the township.

He had a good chance still to break free to safety, to ride to the hideout of one of his clandestine, low-life associates. Over his long years in Cox City he'd employed a raft of people who had unsuspected places where he could hole up or gain access to the means to flee this country. Regrettably, he would be quitting the years of effort he'd put into the Magnet, but he'd be away with his life.

The West was still wide and wild. People didn't ask questions of strangers on the frontier; it was a forbidden. Someplace where he couldn't be immediately recognized, he'd start up again from scratch and the suckers would let him make another fortune.

The rush of wind cooled his sweating brow, and an instinct caused him to draw rein and turn his head. Behind him came rapid hoof-falls, and into sight, a lone rider in hard pursuit.

'Dillard!' he shrieked, near-hysterically.

His town council cronies had slipped up

badly in bringing the ex-Pinkerton here. They'd thought he'd prove some kind of town-tamer. *Wrong!* The two-timing son-ofabitch had become a loco killer who delivered his own brand of justice.

The marshal was mounted on another of the animals that had been hitched at the rail across from Axford's Cox City home.

He was implacable, a fiend! A relentless, avenging angel of death...

*Crack! Crack!*

Axford expended his .32 derringer's last shots in futile rage. Fear. He kicked his horse's sides and sent it racing on.

Another mile flashed by and still Dillard gained on him. He became aware of a wet-ness affecting his seat in the saddle. Glancing down, he saw that his pants were soaked in blood down to the knees. Why, the saline reek of it was rising to his nostrils. Only an unfamiliar light-headedness allowed him to ignore the seriousness of his wound. That and the determination to reach a safe haven.

Bleeding copiously, he rode on, another

mile ... two.

He was heading higher up Broken Man Gulch, to where the land was increasingly rugged and the trail crossed the rushing river by a narrow bridge. It felt to him as though his mount were a boat he sailed smoothly through the air on a favourable wind.

'I'll make it ... I'll get clean away,' he told himself, his mind growing steadily more cloudy, yet his spirits oddly calmer.

Blood loss finally claimed his senses as he clattered on to the high timber bridge. The reins slipped through his numbed fingers and his head drooped toward the saddle-horn. Suddenly, he was keeling over sideways in the blood-slippery leather beneath him.

Next moment, totally losing his balance and his seat in the saddle, he toppled from the buckskin's back.

His senses partially returned as he crashed through the splintering bridge rail. Amidst jagged wood slivers that span around him like the spokes of a disintegrating cartwheel, he went on falling.

Far below him was a whirling kaleido-scope of frothing water and black rocks. He let out one high-pitched, continuous scream as the tableau drew rapidly closer ... then, at the last, hurtled up to meet him.

His bloodied body bounced after it hit the rocks, but he didn't know that.

# 15

## THE LAST DISAPPEARING ACT

Joshua rode back to Cox City on his com-mandeered horse. His arm was sore and throbbing, and when a crowd pressed around him at the hitch rack, firing questions about the mysterious morning outbreak of shooti-ng, he brushed them aside curtly.

He felt far from good about the outcome of the wild chase. At bottom, it was no bad thing that a villain of Aces Axford's magnitude was dead. But Joshua swore to himself. His regret was there'd be no trial; little public chance for him to explain his seemingly high-handed actions.

Mayor Miller and his council had, he knew, all been cronies of Axford – the saloon man was to the last well-connected politically. Aces had pulled the wool over the townsmen's eyes in spades. They'd take some convincing of his guilt.

When or if they were, they might adopt the line that it had been a dereliction of his duty not to make an efficient arrest. Coming on top of the deaths of Blackie Dukes and his gang and the rancher Lars Eriksen, it was possible that those who chose to could throw a bad light on his record as Cox City marshal. It wouldn't be fair, or even true – he'd acted promptly and decisively throughout – yet it might be done.

But maybe this wouldn't matter – at least he had Kate Thompson and Hannah Powell to give a true report on the violence at the Eriksen ranch.

Joshua climbed the stairs to his office. Deputy Mahoney had coffee brewing and he poured himself a mug and plumped himself down in a swivel chair. As the seat turned, the barred cell fronts in the adjoining chamber came partially into his view.

Every cell was empty.

'Hey!' he cried, leaping up again. 'Where's Kate Thompson, Deputy?'

'She went, Mr Dillard.'

'What do you mean, she went?'

'I guess she had a change o' female mind, Marshal,' Mahoney said, at a loss over Joshua's agitation.

'But I needed her as a witness to the deaths at the Eriksen place. Where did she go? Not back to that bastard of a husband, surely?'

Mahoney shuffled uncomfortably and shrugged his shoulders. 'Naw, a reunion with Betzinez weren't part o' the pitcher she gave me, though she never said. Have I done wrong, Mr Dillard? Yuh did say she weren't no prisoner, and she was adamant she wanted to go out. Yuh know how a lady can be when she gets a notion...'

Joshua raised his eyes in vexation – and what should happen but that they fell on the high shelf where he'd deposited Ramon Betzinez's suit that Kate had worn so baggily.

It, too, was gone.

'Oh, my God,' he groaned. 'I'm starting to have a real bad feeling.'

Mahoney said tentatively, 'I reck'n I saw Miss Kate head toward the Magnet when she left, Mr Dillard. Could be she's thar if'n yuh want her.'

Far from being encouraged, Joshua was thrown into a still deeper state of alarm. A fresh and more horrible suspicion was dawning on him.

'Hold the fort, Mahoney! I gotta get over to the Magnet pronto!'

The Magnet had not opened for the day's business when Joshua burst through the batwings. Chairs were still up on tables, gambling tables were under dust covers, and bar staff were sweeping up the mess of the previous night's aborted merriment.

A barkeep paused in his sweeping to lean on the broom handle. He gave Joshua the flinty look of the long-suffering; said impatiently, 'We're closed till eleven, Marshal. What can we do for you?'

Joshua went straight to the point of his call. 'Has Miss – Honeydew been here, 'keep?'

'Why, 'deed she has. How did you know that?' The man's surprise made him more forthcoming. 'Almost didn't recognize her first-off, on account of the head-scarf she was wearing. Seems a shame to tie up an' hide all that beautiful blonde hair she's got. She looked kinda – well, bruised up some, too, I guess.'

'Top marks for observation,' Joshua said. 'But more importantly, what did she want and where is now?'

'She went through to get something from her dressing-room, she said... Hey, that's more'n a half hour back.' The thought struck the 'keep as passing strange. 'Can't say that I've seen her since, now that–'

But Joshua was gone.

He crossed the Magnet's stage and swept through the curtain-concealed door at the rear. He'd no reason left to suppose that the rest of his hunch wasn't going to work out exactly as he feared. If he could have placed a bet on it, he would have.

Just as he'd envisioned, he found the door to Axford's private office unfastened. Plainly, it had been inexpertly forced; the splintered frame told him that. Inside the smoke-smelling room, more confirmation screamed the remainder of the story.

The heavy desk had been dragged or shoved about a foot out of position at one end. Joshua wondered where the very feminine Kate Thompson had found the muscle to make such exertion possible. He'd heard that where the will was strong enough, astonishing feats became possible. On the evidence here, maybe he could believe it.

On top of the shifted desk, sitting incongruously among the pens, the wire baskets of papers and Axford's massive glass ashtray, was a pile of discarded women's clothing. Joshua recognized garments that had been loaned to Kate by Hannah's town friend.

Beside the desk, a square of carpet had been lifted from a place where it had been partly covered by the positioning of the desk. If a person had known to look, the cuts in the carpet would probably have always been obvious. Now the carpet piece was tossed aside, a corresponding section of floorboards could be seen to form a kind of trapdoor.

Joshua lifted it out. The locked metal strongbox that had allegedly been Axford's alternative to using his obvious office safe wasn't there. Nor had he expected it to be.

What unexpectedly was there – at the bottom of the mockingly empty gaping aperture – was a sealed envelope with his own name, *Joshua Dillard*, inscribed on it in copperplate handwriting.

He recognized the hand as the same as

had penned the note once thrown through Deputy Steve Wye's window. The envelope matched a rack of similar unused envelopes on the desktop.

Kate, it seemed, had availed herself of Axford's stationery as well as his hidden loot.

Dust and more of the stale tobacco stink rose as Joshua dropped, exasperated, into the dead man's well-padded desk chair and quickly ripped the letter open with a bone paper-knife. He drew out and unfolded a crackling sheet.

Kate's letter was in the same neat handwriting as the envelope. But Joshua noted that in the last of its three succinct paragraphs the writing deteriorated rapidly. It read:

*Dear Mr Millard*
*I must ask your pardon for my ill-mannered behaviour in rejecting your kind hospitality and once again taking advantage of your nature,*

which is that of a true gentleman. I fear I can find the courage neither to endure more of life with my lawful husband, Mr Ramon Betzinez, nor to fight him in the courts. I wish I could write faster, for I shall never be able to tell you all I have got to say before it is wise to depart from here.

Ramon offered me opportunity and succour when I was in sore need. However, he has long since degenerated into a smug and monstrous bully, living without shame on the earnings of myself, his abused wife and client. At the last, I was a caged songbird retained in a gilded prison purely for the attribute of my voice.

I can abide so very miserable a situation no longer, and will therefore make good use of Mr Aces Axford's ill-gotten riches to establish myself yet again in a new identity in a civilized place where Ramon will not find me. Likewise, this place shall be far from the unloveliness of Cox City, of which I find I have only harsh memories. It is also a violent and thoroughly hypocritical community which I would urge you yourself to shun forthwith. Goodbye, Mr Dillard, I hope you

*will not think too badly of me.*
    *Yours respectfully*
    *Kate Thompson*


Joshua refolded the letter, put it back in the envelope and into a coat pocket. He was boiling with wrathful indignation. Kate Thompson had outwitted him again! And in the very same territory as seven years previously. Didn't she realize she'd exposed him to derision. He'd be ridiculed; made a laughing-stock.

Or would he? If he hurried, he might be able to thwart the young woman's schemes even at this late stage, and salvage his career as Cox City's lawman.

Kate followed a pattern when she donned disguise and pulled her disappearing acts, didn't she?

Nodding to himself knowingly, he thrust himself to his feet and stormed out of the plundered office. 'The livery!' he said aloud and two women passing by with baskets on their arms started and gave him a strange look.

Curtis Reisman, as luck would have it, was working a double shift. The hostler greeted Joshua with a bored yawn.

'Might've known yuh'd be along. Soon as that young feller came in ag'in – the one you was askin' after this mornin'. Didn't yuh find him?'

Joshua's temper snapped. 'He's not a him – he's a *her*. A cheat, a liar and a thief! A woman in men's duds, you fool!'

Reisman was not unduly impressed by the revelation. Nor even Joshua's anger. He liked his women obvious and the men he had to do business with placid. His brows knitted and he cuffed his nose with a dirty sleeve.

'Yuh don't say. Why it's ag'inst the law to dress improper to your sex.'

'You're a mine of information, hostler.'

'Sure I am, Marshal. She's not long gone. Might still be in your bailiwick. Ain't yuh gonna chase after her?'

Joshua emitted a long groan of exasperation. 'Again...! Maybe I will; maybe I won't.'

But Reisman nodded to himself sagely. 'That's what a lawman oughta be for – arresting lawbreakers. 'Specially sassy lawbreakers who can't talk to a body with a civil tongue.'

'What did she say?' Joshua demanded.

'Tol' me to mind m' own business 'bout the great metal box she was totin'.' He treated Joshua to a surly scowl as he remembered. 'Wouldn't so much as let me touch it.'

Joshua made up his mind. 'Which way did she ride?'

'This time she kinda headed for the stage road east.'

The only reply Joshua made was an abrupt nod. It was all the thanks he could bring himself to give for the liveryman's story.

He went back to the courthouse office. His deputy had pinned a message on the locked door. *'Gone to lunch – back in five minutes. Mahoney.'*

Joshua went to rip it off, but changed his mind.

220

He unlocked the office and went in. He emptied his desk drawers and stuffed personal belongings into his warbag. Then he unpinned the big tin star from his coat and tossed it in the wastepaper basket.

'Never did like the damn' flashy thing anyway,' he muttered under his breath. 'Too official-looking. And that ain't my style these days.'

Deputy Mahoney, true to his lax ways, had still failed to reappear. On his way out, Joshua took out a pencil and scrawled under Mahoney's note: *'Gone for ever. Tell Mayor Miller he can keep my final pay. Joshua Dillard.'*

A little later, badgeless, near moneyless, Joshua took the trail out of Cox City. Sometime during the past half-hour, he'd decided he didn't want to be a lawman, and didn't begrudge Kate the songbird her latest fresh chance – not when the only justification would be his hurt pride.

He would mount no pursuit this time. Kate Thompson deserved to keep Aces Axford's ill-gotten gains as much as anyone.

221

As a man of conscience, he'd realized this was justice. It was unconventional, but it was true to his personal principles, and more appropriate than any other feasible outcome.

The trail he chose for himself led not east but west under a cloudy sky where the sun was already past its zenith, sinking toward the jagged line of the purple mountains.

The publishers hope that this book has given you enjoyable reading. Large Print Books are especially designed to be as easy to see and hold as possible. If you wish a complete list of our books please ask at your local library or write directly to:

**Dales Large Print Books**
Magna House, Long Preston,
Skipton, North Yorkshire.
BD23 4ND